ADVENTURES IN HISTORY ®
THE BATTLE OF THE BULGE

STEPHEN W. SEARS is the author of numerous books of military history, including six award-winning books on the Civil War, among them, *Landscape Turned Red*. *The New York Times Book Review* has called him "arguably the pre-eminent living historian of the war's eastern theater." He is a former editor of American Heritage.

D1455560

THE BATTLE OF THE BULGE

STEPHEN W. SEARS

Consultant
S.L.A MARSHALL, Brigadier General, USAR, Ret.
Chief Historian, European Theater of Operations

ibooks

www.ibooks.net

DISTRIBUTED BY SIMON & SCHUSTER, INC.

An ibooks, inc. Book

Distributed by Simon & Schuster, Inc.
1230 Avenue of the Americas, New York, NY 10020
ibooks
24 West 25th Street
New York, NY 10010

The ibooks World Wide Web Site address is:
www.ibooks.net

ISBN: 0-7434-9333-8
First ibooks printing December 2004
10 9 8 7 6 5 4 3 2 1

PRINTED IN THE U.S.A.

CONTENTS

FOREWORD

In mid-December, 1944, Americans heard on their radios and read in their newspapers the most shocking war bulletins since the Japanese surprise attack on Pearl Harbor almost exactly three years before. Under the headline GERMANS DRIVE 18 MILES INSIDE BELGIUM, one paper reported: "The German high command hurled thousands of crack troops and large numbers of tanks into the great fluid battle that may decide the course of World War II.... Front-line officers of the United States First Army made no attempt to minimize the seriousness of this effort...."

The shock of the news was so great because it was so unexpected. Nazi Germany was thought to be all but finished. Since their landings in France the previous June, the Anglo-American armies had compiled a record of unrelieved victory. On December 16 they were preparing a massive drive toward the Rhine River that promised to break the back of Nazi resistance on the Western Front. But on that day, in the foggy dawn, the German Army counterattacked with the fury of a thunderbolt. The result was the great Battle of the Ardennes—or to give it its popular name, the Battle of the Bulge.

This narrative, reinforced by battlefield photographs, sketches, and paintings, describes that immense fight in the wooded hills and deep valleys of the Ardennes. It was a brutal, bloody struggle in a dismal winter landscape against an enemy imbued with Adolf Hitler's fanatic conviction that victory could be snatched from defeat.

The Bulge was the United States Army's greatest and fiercest battle of World War II. Over a million men and thousands upon thousands of guns and tanks and other fighting vehicles were engaged. In that "dark December," fighting against heavy odds, the American soldier faced his strongest challenge of the European war. This is the story of that challenge and how it was met.

The Editors of
American Heritage

I

CHRISTROSE

On December 12, 1944, thirty German generals were summoned from the battlefront to the city of Koblenz, on the Rhine River fifty miles east of the Belgian border. They had no clue to the reason for the summons—except that it came from the Führer himself. As soon as it was dark, the generals were herded aboard a bus at Koblenz military headquarters and driven aimlessly for half an hour along twisting back roads in the rain until they became thoroughly lost. Finally the bus stopped near a gaunt medieval castle, and they were marched between rows of guards into a massive concrete bunker built into the side of a hill. This was Adlerhorst—Eagle's Eyrie—Adolf Hitler's secret command post on the Western Front.

Hard-eyed guards of the SS (the Schutz-staffel, or military arm of the Nazi party) brusquely relieved the generals of their briefcases and pistols. In a conference room they were seated in ranks, their chairs carefully spaced three feet apart. Armed SS men posted around the room watched them intently. "No one in the audience dared move or even take his handkerchief out of his pocket," one of the officers later recalled. When Hitler made his entrance his appearance visibly shocked the generals. His body was stooped, his face was flaccid and pale, his left arm twitched violently and uncontrollably. As he walked he dragged one foot.

Thus the nerve center of Nazi Germany in the sixth year of World War II: a dank underground headquarters obsessed with security, a cowed and humiliated army high command, and absolute ruler over all, the broken, shuffling figure of the Führer of the German Third Reich.

That the once-mighty Nazis had fallen to such a sorry state was perhaps not surprising in view of the critical war situation. Hardly more than two years earlier they were the bloody-handed masters of nearly all of Europe. Now they were like cornered rats, their backs to the wall. But the grim scene at Eagle's Eyrie also reflected something else—the attempt five months before by a group of army officers to kill Hitler to end a war they believed was hopelessly lost.

On July 20, 1944, Colonel Klaus von

Stauffenberg had used his briefcase to smuggle a bomb into just such a conference as this one. The Führer was only wounded by the explosion, however. In the savage bloodbath that followed, Stauffenberg and hundreds of plotters and suspected plotters were butchered by the SS and the Gestapo, the Nazi secret police.

Hitler saw his survival as a miraculous sign from Destiny, fresh proof that he was chosen to lead Nazism to ultimate victory and supremacy over the Western world. His escape from death, he told the nation in a radio broadcast the day after the assassination attempt, was "the guiding hand of Providence directing that I must, and will, carry out my task." To his advisors, he confided that the German people would have to prove themselves worthy of his vision. If they failed, they deserved to be utterly destroyed. There was no middle course.

The Führer began to address the Adlerhorst conference in a low, hesitant voice, using no notes. For an hour and a half he rambled on, ranging through Germany's history and the history of the Nazi party. As he had done often in the months since the July Plot, he turned to his favorite historical figure, Frederick the Great. During the Seven Years' War in the eighteenth century, Frederick led Prussia, the parent-state of modern Germany, to victories against great odds. In the end his boldness had been rewarded by the collapse of the coalition of nations opposing him.

"People may say: Yes, but then the situation

was different," Hitler said. "It was not different, gentlemen! At that time all his generals, including his own brother, were near to despairing of success. His Prime Minister begged him to put an end to the war since it could no longer be won. The steadfastness of one man made it possible for the battle to be carried through...."

Hitler left no doubt as to whom he considered the twentieth-century Frederick the Great.

As he warmed to his subject, some of his old zeal began to return. The stooped figure straightened, the dulled eyes came alive. Here again was the spellbinding orator who had whipped up the massed audiences at Nazi party rallies before the war, those huge terrible spectacles that left the watching world uneasy.

Hitler turned to the coalition now arrayed against Germany. The British, the Americans, and the Russians, he claimed, represented "the greatest opposites which exist on earth." What each hoped to gain from the war made them at heart enemies rather than allies—the British sought to hold onto their dying empire at any cost, the Americans sought to take over that empire, the Russians sought the destruction of the two democratic states in the name of Communism. "These antagonisms grow stronger and stronger from hour to hour," he said. "If now we can deliver a few more heavy blows, then at any moment this artificially constructed common front may suddenly collapse with a gigantic clap of thunder...."

The first of these "heavy blows" was about

to fall on the Western Front, the Führer told his startled listeners. The three armies in which the generals held command would soon attack in an area known as the Ardennes, the sector of the front straddling the Belgian border due west of Koblenz. Utilizing total surprise, shielded from the powerful Allied air forces by bad weather predicted for December, they would slice through the thin American line in the Ardennes and turn northwest. Their objective was to split apart the two wings of the Allied forces and seize Antwerp, the great Belgian port upon which they depended for most of their supplies. The Allied northern wing then would be ripe for annihilation.

Without their air power the Americans had no stomach for fighting, Hitler insisted; once through the front-line positions, the German assault troops would find nothing to oppose them but hapless cooks and mechanics, led by bank clerks trying to be officers. It would be the French campaign of 1940 all over again: then German tanks had plunged through the Ardennes and all the way to the English Channel, splintering the British-French coalition, demoralizing the French Army and driving the British off the Continent.

The great new offensive, code-named Operation Christrose, would begin in four days. "It will not be possible to concentrate so much equipment a second time," Hitler warned. "If we fail we face dark days...."

The conference ended with the officers filing past their Führer for a final word of encouragement. Several took the opportunity to request changes in the plan. Hitler was short with them: no changes would be permitted. Christrose would be carried out precisely as he had outlined it, and it would be launched as scheduled on December 16 unless there was a break in the forecasted bad weather. As the generals left Eagle's Eyrie to return to their divisions, it was still raining.

The seed of the idea for a counter-offensive on the Western Front had taken root in Hitler's mind in the late summer of 1944—less than a month after the attempt on his life. It was an unlikely time to be planning an attack of any sort. The armies of Nazi Germany were on the run and dangerously close to complete defeat. In the East the Russians had swept into Poland and the Balkans. On the Southern Front German troops were evacuating Greece and Albania to avoid being cut off, and in Italy they were taking up the last good defensive position on the peninsula. In the West the situation was even more desperate. The British and Americans had exploded out of their beachhead in Normandy and with seven-league strides had liberated Belgium, Luxembourg, and most of France, threatening Germany's industrial heart in the Ruhr Valley.

All told, the summer campaigns had swallowed up seventy-eight Nazi divisions—some one and a half million men and all their equipment. In the air the Anglo-American bombing campaign against the cities and industries of the Third Reich went on at a furious pitch; German production of oil and gasoline, the lifeblood of a modern army, was down seventy-five per cent by September.

Confronted by this catalogue of disaster, Hitler stunned his top military advisors at a conference in mid-September by pounding the map table with his fist and exclaiming: "I have made a momentous decision. I am taking the offensive. Here—out of the Ardennes! Across the Meuse and on to Antwerp!"

This was the sort of decision, flying in the face of all logic, that only a totalitarian dictator could make. It was a decision that Adolf Hitler, in his utter confidence that Providence had spared him from the assassin's bomb to lead the Third Reich back from the abyss, hesitated not at all to make.

As the autumn weeks passed, Hitler's strategy of counterattack suddenly began to look at least possible. On all fronts the German armies managed to hold. Stubborn resistance and bad weather—the worst in Europe in fifty years—combined with overextended supply lines to stall the Allied armies. Thanks to the skillful efforts of War Production Minister Albert Speer and the foul weather that hampered the Allied bombers, German industry made a comeback.

In the Allied view this autumn stalemate was merely a pause before the final storm that soon would destroy the Nazi cancer infecting Europe. In point of fact, it gave Hitler the chance to make one final cast of the dice, one last gamble to avert defeat.

The Nazis desperately needed to regain the

initiative in order to gain time—time to mass-produce their array of new and very deadly weapons beginning to come into action in the fall of 1944. These included jet- and rocket-powered fighter planes capable of wrenching control of the air from the Allies; fast, deep-diving submarines to menace the "bridge of ships" bringing men and supplies from the United States to Europe; and V-2 rocket missiles to spread havoc in the cities of Britain and the Continent.

Logic demanded that the counter-offensive take place in the West. On the vast Eastern Front, even if a breakthrough were made, there were no vital objectives within reach. The Russians would simply pause briefly to make good their losses from a seemingly inexhaustible supply of men and come on again. It was different in the West. Operation Christrose, if it succeeded, would seize the Allies' main supply port within a week and cut off some twenty-five divisions in Belgium and Holland.

Such a blow, Hitler promised his high command, would take the fight out of the "decadent democracies." The British already had been bled white by the long and costly struggle. Surely the Americans, fighting more than 3,000 miles from their homeland, would give up their demand for unconditional surrender in favor of a negotiated settlement of a war that did not directly concern them anyway. Then the Third Reich could turn its full attention to the Russian menace.

Thus Christrose was born in the twisted mind

of Adolf Hitler. It was a plan conceived with cunning, militarily risky but politically vital, based on a wildly optimistic estimate of the temper of the enemies he was facing.

Hitler's enemies, for their part, were not doing a very good job of estimating the opposition they faced either. By December the Anglo-American high command believed that it had regained the momentum lost during the autumn stalemate. Its armies had closed to the Siegfried Line, the main German defensive position in the West, and at one point, at Aachen, north of the Ardennes, they had punched a large hole in it. Supply difficulties had been largely overcome, and orders were laid on for a major push to reach the Rhine River, the final natural barrier in the West.

"It is now certain that attrition is steadily sapping the strength of German forces on the Western Front," read an Allied Intelligence report issued on December 12—the same day that Hitler announced his attack plans to the generals at Eagle's Eyrie. "The crust of defenses is thinner, more brittle and more vulnerable than it appears...to the troops in the line." Another Intelligence bulletin went so far as to predict that a German collapse "may develop suddenly and without warning."

The Allied Supreme Commander, Dwight D. Eisenhower, had three powerful army groups under his command. In the north was British Field Marshal Bernard Montgomery's 21st Army Group, composed of the Second British Army and the First Canadian Army. In the center was the 12th Army Group of American Lieutenant General Omar Bradley; under Bradley were the U.S. First, Third, and Ninth armies. To the south, the U.S. Seventh and French First armies made up the 6th Army Group, under American Lieutenant General Jacob Devers. All told, there were fifty Allied divisions spaced along the 500-mile front from Switzerland to the North Sea.

Inevitably, as a stream flows around a rock, the main thrusts of the Allies had bypassed the hilly, forested Ardennes region, located at roughly the midpoint on the Western Front. The Ardennes lay within the zone of Bradley's 12th Army Group, which used it as "a nursery and old folks' home"—that is, as a quiet place to break in new units and to rest combat-weary ones. Since the German defenders did very much the same thing, the Ardennes was a "ghost front," a lightly held area where nothing much happened and where a new soldier could learn his trade and a veteran could take a breather.

Most of the Ardennes sector was the responsibility of Major General Troy Middleton, whose VIII Corps was the weakest of the three corps making up the American First Army. Of Middleton's three infantry divisions, one was brand-new to war, having arrived at the front only on December 12. The other two, badly cut up in fierce fighting along the Siegfried Line to the north, were there for the frank purpose of rest and recuperation. Middleton also had one third of an armored division in his front line; it too was new and untested. Two infantry divisions along the northern edge of the Ardennes, part of Middleton's neighboring corps, were not under his command.

In all there were only 85,000 men to cover a front of eighty-five miles, a ratio that Middleton did not like at all. The Allied high command was willing to accept this calculated risk in order to strengthen its assault forces on the rest of the front. As General Bradley later put it, "To push on in the attack—or bed down until the spring: these were the alternatives we faced." This was slight comfort to Middleton.

Although American patrols had managed to spot three more enemy divisions than usual opposite the Ardennes, much of the German buildup for Operation Christrose went undetected. No less than twenty divisions, seven of them armored, were moved into position for the attack. Troops and weapons came from as far away as Norway, Poland, East Prussia, and Austria. More than 1,500 troop trains and 500 trainloads of supplies reached the Western Front, moving by night and hiding from Allied planes in forests and tunnels by day. Some 15,000 tons of artillery ammunition and 4.5 million gallons of gasoline were stock-piled at various points behind the front.

The thick forests rimming the Ardennes concealed 1,900 pieces of artillery and 970 tanks and assault guns to be used in peeling back the American front line. The Luftwaffe's Hermann Goering promised to support Christrose with a thousand planes, including eighty of the new jet fighters. German generals, who had seen precious little of the once-invincible German Air Force since the Allies landed in France, counted more on bad weather than on Goering's promises to keep Allied fighter-bombers off their necks.

The Germans could not hope to conceal entirely the movement of a quarter of a million men and their heavy equipment from an enemy that had control of the air. But they did hope to fool the Allies about the purpose of the build-up. In this they were entirely successful.

To ensure secrecy, only a handful of top Nazi staff officers and field commanders knew of Christrose and took part in its complex planning. No deception was too small: issuing the troops charcoal so that smoke from wood-burning cook fires would not reveal their hiding places; carefully brushing out vehicle tracks leading into places of concealment; transmitting false radio messages to non-existent units. Larger deceptions also were effective. Train-loads of new tanks, for example, traveled toward other parts of the Western Front in daylight, then changed direction at night and delivered their cargo to the Ardennes. All these efforts were made doubly effective by bad weather that hampered the Allies' reconnaissance planes.

Allied Intelligence officers were left with very little to go on. Their best guess was that the Nazis were massing forces to meet the threat to the Ruhr industrial centers. (Before they were let in on the secret, most German front-line generals made the same guess.) As late as December 10, the daily Intelligence report to Eisenhower's headquarters had to admit: "There is no further news of the Sixth Panzer Army beyond vague rumors." Hitler had assigned the main role in Christrose to the Sixth Panzer Army.

These deceptions contributed much to the Allied Intelligence failure. Even more important was the conviction that the war was nearly over, that Germany was too demoralized, too battered to muster up *any* major counteroffensive. Finally, the Allies were unaware of the iron grip that Hitler had taken on the German Army following the July Plot on his life. Intelligence operated on the assumption that the enemy in the West was being directed according to sound military principles by the man supposed to be in charge, Field Marshal Gerd von Rundstedt.

The wily old Rundstedt had spearheaded the victorious campaign against France in 1940, and his equally skillful management of the autumn battles of 1944 led the Allies to admit ruefully that he had not lost his touch. It seemed inconceivable that he would squander his dwindling reserves in a counterattack anywhere but at the points of most danger to the Third Reich—in the north around Aachen to protect the vital Ruhr or in the south in the Saar region, where the American Third Army was threatening to break through. This was the way the military textbooks said it should be done, and Gerd von Rundstedt was a textbook soldier.

Christrose, however, sprang from the fevered will and intuition of Adolf Hitler, not from any military text-book. When Rundstedt and his staff first saw the plan, they were aghast at its ambitions. "This damn thing hasn't got a leg to stand on!" one of his generals complained. But their every attempt to modify or redirect it was met with a blunt "not to be altered" scrawled in Hitler's handwriting across the planning papers. Allied Intelligence was not alone in being unable to divine the Führer's reasoning.

As December 16 approached, the German build-up took on its final shape. Field Marshal Walther Model, able and energetic, a veteran of the great battles on the Eastern Front, was in operational command under Rundstedt. The main thrust was to be delivered by the Sixth Panzer Army, heavily weighted with elite SS units, attacking with five infantry and four armored divisions in the northern part of the Ardennes. The Sixth's commander was General Josef "Sepp" Dietrich, a crude, hard-drinking one-time butcher and street brawler who was an old crony of Hitler's. Dietrich had a reputation of being more courageous than intelligent. He was a fervent and loyal Nazi, however, a quality especially important to the Führer after the July Plot.

In the center was General Hasso von Manteuffel's Fifth Panzer Army, containing three armored and four infantry divisions. The short, wiry Manteuffel, a polished Prussian aristocrat from an old military family, highly expert in training and handling armored formations, presented a sharp contrast to the hulking Dietrich.

The southernmost force, the German Seventh Army, was assigned a blocking role—guarding Manteuffel's left flank against American counterattacks expected from the south. Its four infantry divisions were led by General Erich Brandenberger, a small, balding, potbellied soldier who was careful and meticulous, well suited to carry out his unspectacular but vital mission.

During the cold and drizzly night of December 15 the German assault forces crept into their jumping-off positions. Straw was laid on the roads to muffle the sound of tank tracks and gun carriages. V-1 robot bombs aimed at Antwerp streaked overhead, drowning out the noise of truck motors. Ramps for vehicles were put in place over the concrete obstacles of the Siegfried Line.

While he waited, one of Dietrich's SS troopers dashed off a letter to his sister: "I write during one of the momentous hours before we attack, full of excitement and expectation of what the next days will bring.... Some believe in living but life is not everything! It is enough to know that we attack and will throw the enemy from our homeland. That is a holy task...."

At midnight a final message from Field Marshal Rundstedt was read to all units: "Soldiers of the Western Front! Your great hour has come. Large attacking armies have started against the Anglo-Americans. I do not have to

tell you more than that. You feel it yourself.
We gamble everything! You carry with you the
holy obligation to give all to achieve super-
human objectives for our Fatherland and our
Führer!"

Earlier in the day, the Intelligence summary
issued by Eisenhower's headquarters routinely
noted. "There is nothing to report on the
Ardennes Front."

II

BREAKTHROUGH

The Ardennes in winter has the look of an old-fashioned Christmas card—steep hills crowned with forests of fir trees, narrow winding rivers, and picture-book villages and quaint old stone castles tucked into deep valleys. To German Field Marshal Walther Model, however, ordered to drive a quarter of a million men and thousands of tanks, trucks, and guns through the Ardennes in a matter of days, there was nothing charming about it at all. It was simply a headache.

Ironically, it is precisely because its terrain is so difficult that the Ardennes has a long military history. Three times—in 1870, in the Franco-Prussian War; in 1914, at the beginning of World War I; and in 1940, early in World War II—France was caught napping by surprise

German assaults through the Ardennes. The French never expected their enemy to pick the hardest possible route of attack—and they never learned anything from the experience. In 1944 the Allies showed that they had not learned the lessons of history either.

The problem of crossing this rugged landscape was made even more difficult for Model because he was aiming directly "against the grain" of the country. The Ardennes covers part of Luxembourg and most of the lower corner of Belgium that separates Germany from France. It is a region of uneven hills and ridges, cut by deep gorges through which rush small swift rivers. The general direction of the ridges is northeast-southwest; if Hitler's armies wanted to reach Antwerp, they would have to go in a northwesterly direction, against rather than with the terrain.

Directly in front of the German jumping-off positions was the deep valley of the Our River. Beyond the Our a number of smaller rivers lay across their path, the most important being the Ourthe, about halfway through the Ardennes. Some sixty miles from the Our, on the western edge of the Ardennes, is the Meuse River. Northwest of the Meuse the country flattens out, allowing a clear sixty-mile run to Brussels and Antwerp for fast armored columns.

The roads in the Ardennes were as narrow and crooked as the rivers, full of hairpin curves and steep grades. The main roads were macadam, the secondary roads poorly paved or not paved at all. There was not a single good highway that went straight through the Ardennes in the direction in which the Germans wanted to go.

The German generals recognized that the battle they were about to make would be essentially a fight for crossroads and bridges. Their main weapons would have to be surprise and speed, their main ally bad weather. Hitler's timetable for victory called for the Meuse to be crossed during the fourth day of the offensive.

On Saturday, December 16, 1944 the predawn stillness of the Ardennes was shattered abruptly by a thunderous cannonade from 1,900 German guns. High-arcing mortar shells thudded around the American outposts. Command posts and artillery positions were blasted by assault guns and rocket batteries. Heavy cannon mounted on railroad flatcars hurled great 14-inch shells into supply depots far behind the lines. The telephone cables laid to the American front-line troops were ripped apart, and when the GI's tried to use their radios to report the attack, they found their wave lengths "jammed" by broadcasts of German band music.

Then, from their hiding places, thousands of German assault troops rose up and began to move forward. Their way was lighted by searchlight beams bounced off the low-hanging clouds. In the pale light and the drifting white ground mist, the advancing figures seemed to waver, disappearing and reappearing—ghosts on a ghost front. Flights of the Führer's new jet fighters shrieked overhead at terrific speeds.

Their morale sent sky-high by the sight, the German troops cheered and began to run.

In their first rush the Germans overwhelmed many of the American outposts, but as the GI's recovered from their surprise they fought back savagely. A series of small, sharp clashes erupted all along the front. A U.S. reconnaissance platoon of eighteen men blocked a key road throughout the day against repeated attacks by a full battalion of German assault troops. In a log forester's hut a lone GI, name unknown, "raised hell with the Krauts" to break up another attack. At a railroad stop called Buchholz Station a company of U.S. infantrymen counterattacked German troops taking cover behind a string of freight cars and a locomotive roundhouse. With mortars and a single tank destroyer—an antitank gun mounted on a tank chassis—they raked the freight cars and sent the enemy scurrying. Sergeant Savino Travalini blew open the roundhouse with a rocketfiring bazooka and then grabbed his rifle to shoot down the Germans one by one as they tried to escape.

Such actions and dozens more like them blunted the thrust of Sepp Dietrich's Sixth Panzer Army in the northern part of the front, but farther south the Germans found a soft spot. The Losheim Gap, a seven-mile-wide valley slanting southwest from Germany into Belgium, was the boundary line between Troy Middleton's VIII Corps and Leonard Gerow's V Corps. The two corps were patched together by a unit of 900 cavalrymen, a light armored force used for reconnaissance and scouting. As a heavy attack force swarmed over them, the cavalrymen broke under the tide and went streaming to the rear. By 9 A.M. the vital Losheim Gap was wide open to the enemy.

This breakthrough put the U.S. 106th Division to the south in grave jeopardy. The 106th, nicknamed the Golden Lions, was made up of men only recently drafted. They had no combat experience, and in their few days at the front they hardly had time to organize their positions in the Schnee Eifel (Snow Mountains).

General Manteuffel had no intention of sending his Fifth Panzer Army head-on against the rugged Schnee Eifel; instead, he planned to throw a noose of men and guns around it to strangle the 106th Division. Half the noose would be laid through the Losheim Gap to the north. The other half would go south through the smaller Alf Valley, in the middle of which lay the village of Bleialf. German infantry, moving silently in small groups, filtered into Bleialf. The American garrison battled them from street to street and house to house with rifles, machine guns, grenades, and knives. Although the Germans were slowed, it was clear as the day wore on that they were cutting a serious gap in the American line. The noose around the young Golden Lions tightened.

Manteuffel's main interest was not the 106th Division, however. His primary targets were the towns of St. Vith and Bastogne. Both were important road centers, and without the road networks these towns commanded, Operation

Christrose had no chance of reaching the Meuse's real force. As a result, the heavier weight of Manteuffel's army, five divisions, was aimed at the part of the front held by the U.S. 28th Division.

The 28th was as experienced as the 106th was green, but it had been severely mauled in the bloody battle for the Siegfried Line in November where it lost nearly half its 14,000 men. It had been sent to the Ardennes wanting nothing more than to be left alone while it rebuilt its morale and absorbed its replacements. Spearheading the attack on the 28th Division was one of the most famous outfits in the German Army, the 2nd Panzer (Armored) Division, which had been battling the Allies since the Normandy landings the previous June.

Even before the predawn bombardment, Manteuffel had sent small parties of shock troops across the Our River in rubber boats to seize a bridgehead. Flowing like water around American strongpoints, the Germans made steady gains. Villages and roadblocks guarding the chief highways behind the front were surrounded and methodically reduced.

The German infantrymen leading the way did not yet have help from their armor and self-propelled guns, and their advance was costly. At one crossroads, for example, more than a hundred of them were killed in a matter of minutes by a lone American half-track blazing away with its four .50-caliber machine guns.

The delay of the 2nd Panzer Division's tanks put Manteuffel in a cold fury. The attack plan called for his engineers to throw two bridges across the Our River by midmorning on December 16, but there was a foul-up somewhere, and the steel roadway sections for the bridges arrived at the crossing sites before the girders that supported them. The roads leading down to the river were narrow and muddy, and it took almost the entire day to sort out the enormous traffic jam of tanks and trucks and construction equipment and to complete the bridges. Not until late afternoon, as the short winter day ended, did the 2nd Panzer's tanks and assault guns begin to rumble forward.

Although the fighting did not stop with darkness on December 16, the chief tasks on both sides that night were to get units straightened out, measure gains and losses, and make plans for the next day's battle.

If the Germans had not achieved all they had hoped for on the first day of Christrose, they had won some very solid gains of up to five miles. Surprise had been complete, and the weather had remained bad enough to keep Allied planes from interfering. Dietrich's Sixth Panzer Army in the north had made erratic advances, but it was in position to get its tanks rolling on at least some of the roads it needed. The Losheim Gap was acting as a great funnel for both Dietrich's and Manteuffel's forces. The 106th Division, on the Schnee Eifel, was in imminent danger of being cut off, and Manteuffel's armor was poised to drive hard for St. Vith and Bastogne. Erich Brandenberger's Seventh Army, on the left flank, had made the shallowest gains of the three Nazi armies.

Adolf Hitler was delirious with excitement over the first day's progress. He telephoned General Hermann Balck, commanding the army group south of the Ardennes, to tell him the news. "Balck, Balck, everything has changed in the West!" the Führer exclaimed. "Success—complete success—is now in our grasp!"

On the American side the battle was a nightmare of confusion and bewilderment. The suddenness of the stroke and the heavy shelling had short-circuited the chain of command, and officers could get very little solid information. Troops fought in isolation, without orders. Facts were greatly outnumbered by rumors.

It was ten hours before General Eisenhower received word of the German offensive at his headquarters at Versailles, outside Paris. He was with General Bradley, commander of the 12th Army Group, when the first reports came in. Bradley believed it was simply a local spoiling attack, a feint designed to drain strength from General George Patton's offensive in the Saar region to the south.

Eisenhower sensed that there was much more to it than that. "This is no local attack, Brad," he said. "It isn't logical for the Germans to launch a local attack at our weakest point." Acting decisively, he approved reinforcements for the Ardennes. Patton was reached by telephone and told to send his 10th Armored Division northward. A second armored division, the

7th, was ordered to move south from the Aachen sector.

"Well, Brad," Eisenhower said, "you've been wishing for a counterattack. Now it looks like you've got it."

"A counterattack, yes," Bradley replied, "but I'll be damned if I wanted one this big!"

Shortly after 3 A.M. on Sunday, December 17, the roar of airplane engines filled the dark skies over the Ardennes. The German airborne army, which had played starring parts in the Nazi victory march of 1940-41, was about to act out its final role.

In this sixth year of war, however, Germany had very few trained paratroopers left and no specially trained pilots at all to drop them, and the whole operation quickly came unstitched. Just ten of the 105 transport planes reached the proper drop zone near the town of Malmédy, fifteen miles behind the American lines. A dozen pilots became so befuddled in the darkness that they released their paratroopers over the peaceful German city of Bonn, fifty miles away.

The leader of the airdrop, Baron Friedrich von der Heydte, expected to have a thousand paratroopers to seize key road centers and bridges and hold them for Sepp Dietrich. By dawn on December 17, he had assembled less than thirty men. They, and another 200 or so scattered all over the northern Ardennes, were unable to take any of their objectives. They could only try to work their way back to the German lines. Five days later von der Heydte, suffering from exhaustion, frostbite, and hunger, was captured.

Despite this sour beginning, December 17 was a day of many successes for the Germans. Before dawn an armored force from Dietrich's army, under cover of a thick fog, surprised the small American garrison at Honsfeld. "I was in my armored car," a GI told the garrison commander, "when a guy came walking down the road in front of a big vehicle, swinging a flashlight. Biggest damn tank I've ever seen. With a swastika on it." The tank was one of the huge new sixty-ton German Tigers, half the size of the U.S. Sherman tanks.

Honsfeld's capture gave the Germans their first open road westward. SS Colonel Joachim Peiper immediately ordered his armored kampfgruppe (battle group) to roll. Striking fast, the tankers overran an American fuel depot and Kampfgruppe Peiper paused to fill up its gas tanks. Then, at 9 A.M., it hurried on again, spurred by its impatient commander.

At about the same time, ten miles to the south, General Manteuffel knotted his noose around two entire regiments—some 9,000 men—of the 106th Division. The night before, Major General Alan Jones of the 106th had explained his plight to the VIII Corps commander, Troy Middleton. The telephone connection was bad, however, and there was a tragic misunderstanding. Middleton told Jones that reinforcements were on the way but to withdraw if the situation became critical. Jones understood that he was to hold on until the reinforcements arrived. And so the Golden Lions stayed in their foxholes and less than twelve hours later they were surrounded.

By noon on December 17, panic was licking around the edges of the broken American lines. The muddy roads leading westward from the Losheim Gap and the Schnee Eifel were jammed solid with routed men and their equipment. Armored cars, jeeps, ambulances, self-propelled guns, construction vans, cranes, kitchen trucks, and assorted other vehicles ground along bumper-to-bumper, hurrying away from the advancing Nazi tide. Dazed men, some of them without their helmets and weapons, plodded beside the roads and through the soggy fields. The sky was black with smoke from supply depots set afire to prevent their falling into enemy hands.

An American sergeant named Henry Giles, returning from leave to his outfit at Malmédy, recorded in his diary impressions of that grim Sunday. "An MP [military policeman] stopped us and told us all hell had busted loose," Giles wrote. "The Krauts were attacking and the whole country was crawling with them; they were heading for Liège and we'd better get back there as fast as we could. He was shaking like a leaf and it was plain whether it was true or not he believed it.... When I got back here [to Liège] there was much excitement with a lot of rumors. You don't know what to believe and nobody really knows the score here.... Everybody in this place has got the shakes, bad...."

Reports of von der Heydte's paratroopers

triggered some of the rumors that spread like a prairie fire behind the American lines. Most of them, however, were the result of Operation Greif, a special plan devised by Hitler himself. Something over a hundred English-speaking German commandos, wearing American uniforms and driving captured American jeeps, sped through the Ardennes, getting even as far as the Meuse. They cut telephone lines, reported the location of supply dumps, changed signposts, and on at least one occasion, sent American reinforcements in the wrong direction.

The success of Operation Greif was not so much what it actually did but rather, the seeds of confusion and suspicion that it sowed. When one of the commandos was captured and he revealed his mission, rumor production went into high gear. Generals were stopped by privates and forced to answer questions about American baseball teams and movie stars and comic strip characters and even to sing a silly popular song called "Mairzy Doats" to prove that they were not Germans in disguise. Guards swarmed around General Eisenhower —much to his disgust—to protect him from a reported assassination attempt. "Most of these GI-uniformed enemy troops were cut down before they reached the Meuse," General Bradley later wrote, "but not until a half-million GI's played cat and mouse with each other each time they met on the road."

Against this tide of rumor and defeat the U.S. 7th Armored Division clawed its way forward toward St. Vith to reinforce that threatened town. At the head of one of its columns Major Don Boyer drove his jeep through the fields beside the road, angrily trying to clear a path for his tanks. Finally he commandeered a thirty-ton Sherman and charged into the midst of the double row of retreating vehicles, forcing them into the ditch to avoid being crushed.

"Take no orders from any officer, regardless of rank, unless he wears the 7th Armored patch," Boyer told his men. "If anyone gets in the way, run over them!" As the tanks began to edge forward, a sergeant in the retreating column leaped aboard one of the Shermans. "I'm going with these damned tanks!" he shouted. "I'm in this here army to fight, not run!"

"Hi Mac," a tanker greeted him. "You just joined the 7th Armored."

Meanwhile, Kampfgruppe Peiper had burst clear through the American front. Shortly after noon, at a crossroads two miles from Malmédy, it surprised and captured a truck convoy of 7th Armored artillerymen. The GI's were disarmed and herded into an open field. As they stood there, arms raised in surrender, a Nazi soldier in a staff car fired his pistol into the group. Then a machine gun opened up, chopping down the prisoners where they stood. When the firing finally stopped, dead and moaning, writhing wounded lay in blood-spattered heaps. SS men walked among them, kicking at the bodies and shooting through the head anyone who moved.

Eighty-six Americans died on that bloody field; four survived to tell their harrowing tale.

The story of the SS's cold-blooded murder of unarmed prisoners went racing through the Ardennes, and by nightfall GI's in even the most isolated forward positions had heard about the "Malmédy Massacre." Infuriated and vengeful, they vowed to make their enemy pay and pay again for the atrocity.

Behind Peiper's spearhead, American troops were holding desperately to the northern edge of the tear in their line. In the twin villages of Krinkelt and Rocherath the struggle seesawed back and forth as lone GI's with bazookas dueled Dietrich's tanks. When they ran out of bazooka rockets, they improvised. Two infantrymen crept up behind a Tiger, threw gasoline over it, and turned it into an inferno with grenades. Behind the villages, on a range of hills known as Elsenborn Ridge, U.S. artillery poured a deadly fire down on the enemy columns. Along the southern edge of the breakthrough, General Brandenberger's Seventh Army was meeting the same kind of bitter resistance from the U.S. 4th Infantry Division, the Germans paying heavily for every yard they gained.

Bloody Sunday was almost over, but one more act remained. The roads assigned to the 2nd Panzer Division for its drive on Bastogne ran westward from the Our River for eight miles, then plunged and twisted down into a deep valley to cross the Clervaux River at the village of Clervaux. Waiting there for

Manteuffel's tanks was the 28th Division's 110th Regiment, led by a hard-bitten, out-spoken colonel named Hurley Fuller. Fuller's orders were blunt. "Hold at all costs," his division commander told him. "No retreat. Nobody comes back."

Fuller and his men, backed up by a handful of Sherman tanks and a battalion of artillery, tried valiantly to hold. By midafternoon, however, they were being hit from three sides, and at dusk German tanks and infantry reached the streets of Clervaux itself. The remaining Shermans fled. Tank shells and machine guns raked Fuller's headquarters in the local hotel. Firing as they went, the few survivors of the 110th Regiment scattered into the woods and fields beyond the burning town. Fuller and his staff climbed out a back window of the hotel and escaped on foot. (Two days later they were captured.) It was fully dark now, and the 2nd Panzer's heavy tanks blundered through the narrow streets like great clumsy elephants, bumping into buildings and splintering porches.

The capture of Clervaux knocked out the last strong defensive position guarding Bastogne. Twenty-five miles to the northeast, German infantry and armor were closing in on St. Vith, the other key that would unlock the entire American position in the Ardennes.

That evening, east of St. Vith, General Manteuffel came upon Field Marshal Model prowling the battle-field. "Like myself," Manteuffel recalled, "he was on foot, for as a result of the utter chaos on the roads ... it was quicker to walk than to drive." They discussed the pace of the offensive, and Model offered a crack assault brigade to help speed up Manteuffel's attack. "We've got to take St. Vith tomorrow," Manteuffel agreed, "and the brigade may swing the balance."

"Heil Hitler," Model said as they parted. "And good luck tomorrow."

Even as the two German generals made their plans, the mud-spattered Shermans of the 7th Armored Division rolled into St. Vith. It had taken them all day to fight their way sixty miles through the backwash of defeat. The 7th's commander, Brigadier General Robert Hasbrouck, prodded his tired men into defensive positions in a large horseshoe around the threatened town—not a moment too soon. One of the Shermans scored a direct hit on the lead Panther of a probing Nazi armored column. As the Panther exploded in flames, the rest of the German tanks made a quick about-face and retreated.

As Bloody Sunday ended, Operation Christrose was nearly forty-eight hours old. From Monschau in the north to Echternach in the south the Ardennes was aflame. Some fifty German columns were poised to widen and deepen the breach.

By now, too, at American command posts and divisional headquarters, the German penetration was beginning to take a distinctive shape on the situation maps. Before long, almost as if by common consent, it began to be called the Battle of the Bulge.

U.S. Air Force

The German Messerschmitt 262 was the first operational jet fighter. It had a maximum speed of 525 mph and outperformed all Allied fighters, including America's top fighter, the P-51 Mustang which had a maximum speed of 445 mph. The Me-262 was one of Hitler's "wonder weapons" that included the V-1 "buzz bomb" and the V-2 ballistic missile. Hitler believed that these weapons could turn the tide of war in Germany's favor, provided he could win sufficient time to mass produce them. This was one of the reasons behind Operation Christrose.

A Nazi soldier waves his comrades forward. In the background are wrecked American vehicles. This picture is from a film shot by a German cameraman early in the battle.

A Nazi infantryman sprints across a road past an American cannon. The Germans utilized transport they captured to keep their offensive rolling forward.

A GI checks the papers of a truck driver. One of the more successful ploys by the Germans during the Battle of the Bulge was Operation Greif, a German commando raid led by Colonel Otto Skorzeny. English-speaking commandos wearing captured American uniforms and false identity papers infiltrated American lines and attempted to create confusion and havoc. Most of the commandos were caught and shot. The impact of Operation Greif far exceeded the small number of commandos that participated in it. Rumors of disguised German infiltrators swept the theater. Security became so tight at allied supreme commander General Dwight Eisenhower's headquarters that he became a virtual prisoner.

SS troopers of Kampfgruppe Peiper, advancing along the Malmédy road. Colonel Joachim Peiper led 5,000 picked troops in the drive through the Ardennes. When his unit captured the Belgian town of Malmédy, Peiper ordered his men to shoot the 101 Americans they had captured.

GI victims of the Malmédy massacre lie where they fell. Some troops shot in the massacre survived and reported what had happened after they reached American lines. When Malmédy was recaptured, the bodies of the victims were found, tagged for identification, and photographed where they fell. The pictures were used as evidence in the prosecution of Peiper and his men for war crimes in 1946.

U.S. Army Art Collection

Aaron Bohrod painted these tired American troops resting in a church in Berdorf, Luxembourg, a town near the southern edge of the Ardennes. The swift advance of the Allies through France during the summer and fall of 1944 had caused many to believe that Germany was all but finished and that the war would be over by Christmas. Hitler's Ardennes offensive shattered that belief. The Allies would have many more weeks of hard fighting before the war in Europe would end.

Two derelict German Panthers, wrecked by American bazookas, were photographed on a street in Krinkelt on December 17, 1944. The tank in the foreground had its cannon blown off by a direct hit.

Three infantrymen from the 30th Division breaking into a building in the Belgian town of Stavelot to pursue German snipers. The two men at right are carrying rifles adapted as grenade launchers. When the 30th Division captured the town, they cut off Kampfgruppe Peiper's line of retreat.

From left: 12th Army Group commander Lieutenant General Omar Bradley, Supreme Commander General of the Army Dwight Eisenhower, and Third Army commander Lieutenant General George S. Patton, Jr. pose for a picture in the ruins of Bastogne after the Battle of the Bulge. Though Patton was the most junior of the three men, he and his Third Army played the dominant role in the Allied counterattacks during the Battle of the Bulge.

In this German photograph, a Tiger tank heading for the front passes a column of captured American GI's, probably from the decimated 106th Division.

The Belgian town of St. Vith, its buildings devastated, its landscape cratered by bombs and shells, as it looked from the air. After its capture by the Germans, St. Vith was the target of heavy Allied bombing raids.

Paratroopers of the 101st Airborne Division move up to a position near Bastogne. In the foreground is a bazooka team; the lead man is carrying bazooka rockets. When the attack began, the 101st's commander, Major General Maxwell Taylor, was in Washington, D.C. When the division received orders to move to Bastogne and hold the town, the division's artillery commander, Brigadier General Anthony McAuliffe, was named acting commander.

As a shell explodes in the distance, infantrymen from George Patton's Third Army plod across the open fields south of Bastogne in their drive to blunt the German offensive.

Paratroopers of the 101st Airborne sing carols during a Christmas Eve service that was later interrupted by Luftwaffe bombers. "What's merry about all this?" reads a Christmas message to the garrison. "Just this: we have stopped cold everything that has been thrown at us. . . ."

Monks and GI's do laundry together in the courtyard of Bastogne's monastery. During the siege, Combat Command B of the 10th Armored Division used the monastery as its command post. The painting is by Olin Dows.

III

THE FIGHT FOR TIME

In just forty-eight hours Adolf Hitler had plunged the Western Front into a swirling, seething convulsion. The center of violence was the eighty-five-mile Ardennes sector; for a hundred miles in every direction all was frantic motion as masses of men and thousands upon thousands of vehicles rushed toward the whirl-pool.

The element of surprise had served the Germans well—first the sharp surprise of the attack itself, then the numbing, spreading shock at the power behind it. By December 18, the third day of the Battle of the Bulge, field marshals Rundstedt and Model had crowded eighteen divisions into the assault. The U.S. 28th and 106th divisions were battered beyond recognition. In the south the 4th Division's lines were badly buckled. The Americans in the Bulge were desperately short of armor as well as men. In the central sector alone, the day before, sixty tanks had been destroyed by Manteuffel's panzers. Help was on the way, but the odds were poor that it would arrive in time unless somehow the Nazi avalanche could be slowed.

Throughout the Ardennes, at a score of village crossroads, at bridges and in stone barns and in roadside ditches, GI's traded their lives for time. Their orders were everywhere the same: "The Lieutenant said every position was a 'hold fast,'" Sergeant Henry Giles wrote in his diary. "In other words, get killed but don't fall back." Riflemen, tankers, artillerymen—and the mechanics and cooks and clerks that Hitler had scorned as weaklings—stood and fought and won an hour here, a half-day there.

Take, for instance, the stubborn GI's of F Company, 12th Regiment, 4th Infantry Division at the southern rim of the breakthrough. At the first shock of the German assault, the sixty men of F Company had holed up in the Parc Hotel in Berdorf, a resort town in a picturesque area of Luxembourg known as Little Switzerland. The Parc was a three-story hotel that advertised delightful Continental cuisine and "all the modern conveniences"; as far as the besieged GI's were concerned, the Parc's chief conveniences were its sturdy concrete walls and its well-stocked wine cellar.

The Germans succeeded in taking most of the rest of Berdorf, but they had no luck at all dislodging the defenders of the Parc. On

December 18 enemy artillery, mortars, bazookas, and dynamite charges managed to knock off the roof, collapse the top story, and blow gaping holes in the walls; at the same time, American Sherman tanks plastered the hotel with 75-millimeter shells by mistake during an attempted counterattack; but through it all F Company stuck to its guns and denied the enemy the use of the single main road through the town. Berdorf was a mere two miles from the German jumping-off positions in the Siegfried Line, yet it would be five days before F Company gave up its makeshift fortress—and only then on orders to pull back to straighten the defensive lines.

While F Company was being shelled by friend and foe, some fifty miles to the northeast the defenders of the twin villages of Krinkelt and Rocherath were fighting off fresh waves of Sepp Dietrich's SS troops. In the process, Lieutenant Jesse Morrow of the 2nd Infantry Division conducted a one-man war on German Tiger tanks in the streets of Krinkelt.

Morrow knocked out one Tiger by running up behind it and aiming a grenade into an ammunition rack on its rear deck. Not long afterward a second Tiger charged past him and smashed right over an American jeep that blundered into its path. The crash jammed the Tiger's gun turret. It ground ahead, banging its gun barrel against telephone poles to free the turret. Morrow shot a bazooka rocket into the lightly armored rear of the tank, and it spun into a house and then into a ditch. Running forward, he grabbed another bazooka to finish the kill. As he aimed it, he found the huge 88-mm. cannon of the Tiger pointing straight at him, ten yards away. Morrow and the tank gunner fired at the same moment.

The next thing Morrow knew, he was being bandaged at an aid station. "My God," one of the medics was exclaiming, "the Lieutenant here was grazed with an 88 round and he's still alive!"

For another thirty-six hours the defenders of Krinkelt and Rocherath held their ground until their ammunition was gone. Then they pulled out, taking as many of their wounded with them as could be moved. In this savage fight along the northern flank, the U.S. 2nd and 99th divisions each lost more than 2,000 men killed, captured, or wounded. Dietrich had expected to seize the twin villages on the first day of battle; it had taken him four days. And squarely in his path he now faced a second, stronger American defensive line on the vital high ground of Elsenborn Ridge, cobbled together in the time won by men like Jesse Morrow.

One of the most dramatic delaying actions was waged against the German unit setting the pace for the whole of Operation Christrose—Colonel Joachim Peiper's kampfgruppe racing hell-for-leather for the Meuse River.

Peiper's orders were to "drive fast and hold the reins loose," and on December 18 he planned to do just that. Early in the morning, Kampfgruppe Peiper blasted its way through the Belgian industrial town of Stavelot, storming across a big highway bridge before it could be blown up, and headed west. One of its columns, probing up a side road, unwittingly came within a few hundred yards of the American First Army's chief fuel depot, containing 2.5 million gallons of gasoline. But a quick-thinking American major named Paul Solis stacked up a roadblock of gas cans and set fire to it as the leading tank approached. The Germans backed away from the flaming barricade and tried another road.

At 11:30 A.M. the lead tanks of Kampfgruppe Peiper rumbled up to the tiny village of Trois Ponts (Three Bridges), just twenty-five miles from the Meuse. Trois Ponts was a juicy target. Here the Salm and Amblève rivers, twisting through narrow, deep valleys, come together; here, too, all the roads in the area come together, crossing the rivers on arching stone bridges and stretching out invitingly to the west. Once across these bridges, Peiper said later, "it would have been a simple matter to drive through to the Meuse that day."

Guarding Trois Ponts was a company of First Army engineers, 140 strong, armed with rifles, ten machine guns, half a dozen bazookas, and a single 57-mm. antitank gun that had got lost in the confusion and been adopted by the engineers. Twenty-four hours before, these GI's had been operating a sawmill, cutting timber for bridges and fortifications. Few of them had fired their weapons since basic training in the

United States; now they were facing the armored spearhead of the Sixth Panzer Army.

The highway leading down to the bridges twisted beneath a railroad underpass, and the antitank gun was positioned to fire through this narrow opening. The 57-mm. gun all too often had proved about as effective as a peashooter against the big new German tanks, its shells bouncing harmlessly off their heavy armor. But at this critical moment the gunners got off a perfect first shot at the leading Panther. The shell hit the base of its turret, and the Panther slewed sideways across the road and blew up.

For fifteen minutes, while the engineers finished wiring demolition charges on the Trois Ponts bridges, the lone antitank gun held off Peiper's armor. Finally a German shell smashed into the gun and killed all four of its crewmen. As the Germans raced forward, two tremendous explosions erupted right in their faces, and the Salm and Amblève bridges tumbled into heaps of smoking ruins. The main route west was hopelessly blocked.

In a fury Peiper detoured his column northward through the winding Amblève Valley. Some of his SS troopers, however, remained behind to exact a ghastly revenge for their check at Trois Ponts. Twenty-five Belgian civilians—men, women, and children—were hauled from their homes, accused of befriending the Americans, and brutally murdered. An eyewitness wrote of finding "the body of a middle-aged woman who had been stabbed with a knife and then shot. Bodies of two boys between the ages of six and ten were seen with bullet holes in their foreheads.... One old woman had been killed by a smash over the head, probably with a rifle butt...." The sickening list of Kampfgruppe Peiper's atrocities grew longer.

By late afternoon Peiper's round-about detour had brought him near the town of Werbomont, where there was another bridge big enough for his heavy tanks. First Army engineers again made up the bridge guard, a mere squad this time. Corporal Louis Kovacs, a truck driver, tells what happened: "I glanced up and across the bridge I saw a German tank. He stopped at the turn of the road heading for the bridge. His turret was turning and I heard a lot of gunfire. Then I heard this big explosion, saw pink and blue smoke, pieces of timber flying in all directions, and I knew it was the bridge blown."

Peiper was now completely balked. To make matters worse, the weather cleared briefly and he was seen by an American spotter plane. Thunderbolt fighter-bombers pounced on his column, burning out ten tanks and half-tracks and blocking the road. He had no choice but to forget the quick dash to the Meuse that day and double back the way he had come, looking for another opening.

Although he did not yet suspect it, Joachim Peiper's narrowly missed opportunities on December 18 were his last real chances to break clear and cross the Meuse. American reinforcements were beginning to stream into the Ardennes from the north, and Kampfgruppe Peiper soon found itself up against elements of the U.S. 30th Infantry and 82nd Airborne divisions. The fighting was particularly bloody and savage. Meeting the murderers of Malmédy and Trois Ponts, the veteran American infantrymen and paratroopers gave no quarter.

The next day Peiper almost broke through the GI's holding the village of Stoumont, only to be stopped once more, this time by fourteen limping Sherman tanks rounded up from a repair depot. The Germans holed up in a large tuberculosis sanatorium overlooking the town. Their only hope now was to hold on until the Sixth Panzer Army caught up to them.

Meanwhile, the Sixth Panzer's Sepp Dietrich was taking a tongue-lashing from the Nazi high command. Model and Rundstedt, and especially Hitler, wanted to know what was holding up his elite SS army. Except for Kampfgruppe Peiper, the Sixth was far behind schedule.

On the night of Tuesday, December 19, the Führer met at Eagle's Eyrie with Rundstedt and Model. Rundstedt, who had opposed Operation Christrose from the beginning, wanted to call off the offensive. "We have not made the most of our initial surprise," he insisted. "The offensive has never gathered speed, due to the icy roads and the pockets of resistance which forced us to lay on full-dress attacks." F Company at Berdorf and the engineers at Trois Ponts and Lieutenant Morrow in Krinkelt and thousands more like them would have appreciated the compliment.

Model was not yet ready to give up, but he did want the two reserve panzer divisions jammed up behind Dietrich's lagging Sixth Panzer Army to be shifted southward to exploit the breakthrough Manteuffel had made. Hitler, however, still would permit no changes in his plan. He was determined that his loyal old crony Dietrich keep the lead role in the battle. Victory must be won by the "reliable" Nazis of the SS forces, not by the traitorous regular army that had tried to assassinate him. Dietrich's army must keep attacking until it broke through.

Earlier that same day, the American high command had also met. The conference was held in a chilly army barracks in the French city of Verdun.

Supreme Commander Eisenhower opened the meeting on an optimistic note. "There will be only cheerful faces at this conference table," he said. "The enemy has given us a great opportunity.... Instead of having to take the Siegfried Line pillbox by pillbox, we can now beat them by defending the Meuse, while at the same time preparing our own offensive." As Eisenhower outlined it, the Allied strategy would be "to plug the holes on the north and launch a co-ordinated counterattack from the south" with the American Third Army.

The Third Army's George Patton—colorful, profane, impetuous, the best commander of armor in the U.S. Army—burst out that they should let the Germans shoot the works and go all the way to Paris: "Then we'll really cut 'em off and chew 'em up!"

"No, George," Eisenhower replied. "The enemy will never be allowed to cross the Meuse."

Then came the details. Lieutenant General Courtney Hodges would continue to feed every available man and gun of his First Army into the struggle to hold the critical northern flank. Already one of the two American divisions in reserve, the 82nd Airborne, was moving in to help him. The other reserve division, the 101st Airborne, had arrived in Bastogne the night before to try to save that vital road center. Reinforcements from the north and what was left of Middleton's VIII Corps would attempt to blunt the point of the German drive short of the Meuse. Elsewhere on the Western Front, attacks on the Siegfried Line were canceled and forces shifted to cover the gaps left by the reinforcements moving to the Ardennes. All told, a million Allied troops were put into motion.

Eisenhower turned to Patton. "How long will it take you, George, to turn those divisions to the north and attack?" he asked. Patton liked nothing so much as the starring role on a battlefield. He had come to the conference with his plans already made. A few phone calls, he promised, and the Third Army would be on the roads north; inside of forty-eight hours he would be attacking the Bulge. "This time the Kraut has stuck his head in a meat grinder—and this time I've got hold of the handle," he said with a grin.

Patton was as good as his word. By nightfall on the 19th the enormously complex task of pulling six divisions out of the front lines, turning them ninety degrees, and starting their fighting men and tanks and supply convoys on the seventy-five-mile march northward toward the Bulge was well underway. Endless double columns of Third Army vehicles rolled steadily through the night, filling the roads and shouldering through the villages of Luxembourg.

Following the Verdun conference, Eisenhower set about juggling his command set-up. In driving a wedge squarely into the middle of General Omar Bradley's 12th Army Group, the Germans had cut through its delicate network of communications, the central nervous system of modern warfare. Bradley was finding it increasingly hard to maintain control from his headquarters south of the breakthrough. Eisenhower decided to divide the battlefield. Bradley would continue to direct the fighting in the southern half of the Bulge. British Field Marshal Bernard Montgomery, commander of the 21st Army Group, would take over all the forces in the north—including Bradley's U.S. First and Ninth armies.

This was a perfectly logical decision, but it was a bitter pill for many of the American commanders to swallow. Bernard Montgomery, for all his military skills, was a thorny character. He had an abrasive personality that seemed to grate on his American allies; he and Bradley, in particular, struck sparks. Beyond this personality clash there were deeper divisions: U.S. generals thought Montgomery moved too slowly, and Montgomery thought the Americans were too impetuous.

Montgomery's arrival at First Army headquarters on December 20 did not add much to his popularity. "The Field Marshal strode into Hodges' H.Q. like Christ come to cleanse the temple," one of his aides recalled. Refusing the meal offered him, Montgomery spread out a picnic lunch he had brought along and remarked, "Well, gentlemen, I gather that a difficult situation has arisen. Now do tell me the form."

The "form" was still critical. In the south the Battle of Bastogne—described in the next chapter—already had begun; German columns had flowed around and beyond the beleaguered town as far as fifteen miles, and the next day they would surround it. In the center of the battlefield, Manteuffel's three panzer divisions were driving through the gap between St. Vith and Bastogne, steadily extending the Bulge westward. Before the day was out, the 2nd Panzer would make a lucky crossing of the Ourthe River, thirty miles from the Meuse, when demolition charges set by the defenders of the Ortheuville bridge failed to explode.

The tragedy of the U.S. 106th Division was already complete. Trapped on the Schnee Eifel, short of food, without medical supplies for the wounded, nearly out of ammunition, 9,000 of the young Golden Lions had been forced to surrender. "Endless columns of prisoners pass, at first about a hundred, later another thousand," a German lieutenant wrote in his diary. "Now the thing is going. The roads are littered with destroyed American vehicles, cars and tanks. Another column of prisoners passes. I count over a thousand men...."

On the northern flank, however, Sepp Dietrich still was stymied. Hampered by the delay in capturing the twin villages, riddled by the superbly handled American artillery firing from Elsenborn Ridge, the Sixth Panzer Army's line of thrust was being bent from the northwest to the west. This squeezed it up against Manteuffel's neighboring Fifth Panzer Army. Officers of the two armies argued bitterly over the right to use the few available roads. The biggest single problem was the stubborn American grip on St. Vith, for without St. Vith's network of roads, Operation Christrose was doomed to slow strangulation. "It has to be taken fast," Field Marshal Model complained to Manteuffel on December 19. "It's a stumbling block to my whole offensive."

After the arrival late on the 17th of General Hasbrouck's 7th Armored Division, the American defenses of St. Vith gradually were extended in a thirty-two-mile horseshoe-shaped perimeter around the town. Except for the 7th Armored, the defenders were all fugitives from Troy Middleton's battered VIII Corps: the lone surviving regiment of Golden Lions from the 106th Division; a second regiment of infantry, this one from the 28th Division, which had been shattered trying to defend the approaches to Bastogne; and a part of the 9th Armored Division.

For three days this pick-up force, in ever greater danger of being surrounded, beat off enemy thrusts. It was a particularly grim, even demoralizing struggle for the American tank crews. Their Shermans could not match the German Panthers and Tigers in firepower or in armor; in any head-to-head combat the panzers had a clear edge. The only counter was to adopt "Indian tactics." At every opportunity, General Bruce Clarke, commanding the U.S. front-line armor, told his tankers they must fire from ambush or maneuver for a flank shot at the less heavily armored sides and rear of the Nazi tanks. It was a risky business, however, and Clarke's armored strength was steadily whittled down. Desperately plugging one gap and then another, the defenders of St. Vith dug in for the major assault that they knew was coming.

When Field Marshal Montgomery arrived at the headquarters of General Hodges' First Army on December 20, his first impulse was to "tidy up" the battlefield by shifting forces westward and withdrawing from the St. Vith salient. Hodges politely disagreed. Courtney Hodges was a quiet, courtly Virginian, completely lacking the colorful dramatics of a George Patton. But it was his First Army that had been caught napping by the German offensive, and in his quiet way Hodges was determined to avenge the humiliation. In this state of mind, a "voluntary withdrawal," however logical, went against his grain.

Even as the two men argued, a message arrived from St. Vith with the first "hard" information in three days. General Hasbrouck described his precarious position and added, "I can delay them the rest of today *maybe* but will be cut off by tomorrow." That settled the issue. No orderly withdrawal could be made under that kind of enemy pressure; the salient had to be defended.

On Thursday, December 21–the sixth day of the battle–the struggle for St. Vith reached its climax. No more piecemeal attacks: this time the Germans massed more than 10,000 men and 200 tanks, heavily supported by artillery, due east of St. Vith. Just before noon the artillery opened up.

The blistering barrage pinned the heavily outnumbered Americans in their foxholes. Shells burst in the trees overhead, raining jagged shrapnel down on the defenders and killing them by the score. German assault groups of forty or fifty men each crept forward, supported by tanks and self-propelled guns. One by one the defensive strongpoints were overrun as the tanks got in among them and laid down a killing fire with their machine guns. "They're blasting my men out of their holes one by one," an anguished platoon leader telephoned a 7th Armored command post. "Can't you do something to stop'em? Please!"

By 8 P.M. it was fully dark and the American perimeter east of St. Vith was in shreds. The infantry battalion at the point of attack had lost 485 of its 670 men. When five U.S. tanks moved up to try to close the gap, German Panthers fired flare shells into their midst that silhouetted them and blinded their crews in the glare. Within minutes all five Shermans were burning wrecks, picked off like ducks in a shooting gallery. As Nazi tanks and infantry rushed forward into the streets of the town, it began to snow.

St. Vith became a weird inferno. The thickly falling snow softened the red glare of burning buildings and the harsh white light of parachute flares. Tanks and trucks blazed and exploded in the streets. Running figures darted down alleys and from building to building.

A pair of American tank destroyers managed to hold the main street until nearly midnight, when German bazooka fire finally knocked them out. "The men were magnificent, their fire never ceased," recalled Major Don Boyer, who had led the 7th Armored into St. Vith four days earlier. "But always there were more Germans, and more Germans, and then more Germans!"

Through the night the exhausted, dazed defenders who had survived the assault filtered into a new makeshift line west of the town. The U.S. tanks and tank destroyers that escaped came out with scores of infantrymen clinging to their hulls and turrets. Aid men stayed behind with the badly wounded to surrender them to German medics.

The defense of the St. Vith salient had cost the Americans heavily. The 7th Armored Division alone suffered more than 3,300 casualties and lost eighty-eight tanks. But enemy casualties were at least as great; more important, the vital St. Vith road network had been denied to the Germans for five days, winning the time needed to patch the northern edge of the breakthrough.

"They can come back with all honor," Field Marshal Montgomery said of the defenders of St. Vith. "They put up a wonderful show."

IV

BASTOGNE BESIEGED

The Battle of the Bulge was the biggest single battle fought by the United States Army in World War II—and the most confusing. In the memories of Americans who tried to understand what was happening in those dark December days of 1944, the name of Bastogne is special. The heroic defenses of St. Vith and the Elsenborn Ridge area were just as decisive to the final outcome of the struggle; yet Bastogne remains *the* enduring symbol of the American fight against odds in the Ardennes.

It is not hard to see why this is so. Bastogne was a battle within a battle, clearly visible and highly dramatic. It was big enough to be vitally important and small enough to be easily understood. On top of everything else, a memorable remark by the U.S. commander in Bastogne, a remark that ranks with John Paul Jones' "I have not yet begun to fight" in the

Revolution and Oliver Hazard Perry's "We have met the enemy and they are ours" in the War of 1812, has firmly fixed Bastogne in the national memory.

When he first learned of the German counter-attack on the afternoon of December 16, Dwight Eisenhower had ordered two armored divisions, the 7th and 10th, to converge on the Ardennes from north and south to pinch off the penetration. By the next day, however, it was clear that the breakthrough was far too big to be so easily mended. Eisenhower then reached for his only divisions in general reserve on the Continent—the 82nd and 101st Airborne divisions, camped near the French city of Reims.

These were elite divisions, but they had just experienced seventy-two straight days of bitter combat near Arnhem in Holland and they were very battle-weary. Like Troy Middleton's veteran divisions stationed in the Ardennes, they were refitting and training replacements. On the night of December 17 sudden orders came through: mount up and get to the front fast. Someone asked Brigadier General Tony McAuliffe of the 101st what was going on. "All I know of the situation," McAuliffe answered, "is that there has been a break and we have got to get up there."

Since the airborne divisions were set up to go into battle by parachute or glider, just getting them to the Ardennes was going to be a problem. Through the night, supply officers scrounged nearby truck depots and came up with a fleet of big ten-ton trailer trucks. The next day the paratroopers were routed out of their barracks, issued rations and battle gear, and loaded aboard the trucks. There was much grumbling about having to travel just like lowly infantrymen. Everything was in short supply: ammunition, weapons, overcoats, even helmets. There was no time to make good the shortages, and by afternoon the two divisions were on the road.

The Nazis were expecting them. German communications officers tuned in to the Allied radio frequencies were gaining a windfall of information. American radio security was careless, with orders going out uncoded, and the German high command was pleased to learn that Eisenhower's only reserves were now committed to the battle. They calculated that the airborne divisions could not possibly get into action in less than two or three days, too late to do any real good.

However, the airborne commanders—"Slim Jim" Gavin of the 82nd and Tony McAuliffe, running the 101st in the absence of Maxwell Taylor, on leave in the United States—interpreted their orders for speed literally. To collect men and equipment, locate transport, and drive the hundred miles to the battlefield, they allotted just twenty-four hours.

Through the afternoon of the 18th and into the foggy night the long columns of trucks rumbled on. Their headlights blazed, defying the Luftwaffe in order to maintain speed. The men were jammed together in the open trailers, cold and wet and miserable. "The ordeal went on and on," recalled a newspaperman riding with the 101st. "Except for the muffled sound of the engines and grinding gears, the column moved in utter silence. Not a shout was heard.... They crawled along, sunk in a vast coma, a nightmare of misery, despondency, and dread."

The Allied high command intended the paratroopers to take up a blocking position in the center of the Ardennes and seal the breakthrough. But as the battle grew and spread and crisis piled upon crisis, the plan had to be changed. Gavin's 82nd Airborne shifted northward to head off the rampaging Kampfgruppe Peiper. McAuliffe's 101st turned south, to Bastogne.

At Bastogne, as everywhere else on the battlefield, December 18 was a day of desperate scrambling. Somehow, the German spearheads had to be delayed or Bastogne would be overrun before the paratroopers arrived.

As the Screaming Eagles of the 101st hurried eastward toward Bastogne, three German divisions—the 2nd Panzer and Panzer Lehr, both armored, and the 26th Volksgrenadier infantry division—were racing westward toward the same target. General Manteuffel had ordered Panzer Lehr and the Volksgrenadiers to seize the town, allowing the 2nd Panzer to keep driving for the Meuse.

On that critical day, still another force was coming hard on the roads that converged on Bastogne like the spokes of a wheel: Colonel Bill Roberts' Combat Command B of the U.S. 10th Armored Division, rushed up from Patton's army in the south in response to Eisenhower's first call for reinforcements. By the narrowest of margins CCB won the deadly race. Troy Middleton, whose VIII Corps headquarters was in Bastogne, immediately sent Roberts' tanks out to beef up the scrawny VIII Corps roadblocks east of the threatened town. "Move with utmost speed," Middleton told Roberts in his calm Mississippi drawl. "And Robbie, hold those positions at all costs."

These roadblocks of Middleton's had been having a hard day of it. They were strictly pickup affairs, their single purpose to win time. Two of them, each made up of about a dozen tanks and some infantry and named Task Force Rose and Task Force Harper for their commanders, stood squarely in the path of the 2nd Panzer Division that had smashed through Clervaux the night before.

From midmorning until early afternoon on December 18, Task Force Rose fought off the advance guard of the 2nd Panzer, but as the Germans brought up more tanks, Captain L. K. Rose found himself trapped in a cross-fire from three sides. He managed to escape cross-country with a handful of infantry and five surviving tanks. Lieutenant Colonel Ralph Harper's task force was not even that lucky. At dusk the panzers struck like a thunderbolt, piling right through the roadblock and killing Harper and most of his men.

It was a wild, frantic evening in Longvilly, half a dozen miles east of Bastogne. The narrow streets were jammed solid with dazed stragglers from the fighting farther east, Middleton's tanks and artillery were trying to set up to defend the place, buildings were going up in flames under the shelling of German guns, and the whole hellish scene was erratically lit by enemy parachute flares and searchlights. Worst of all, the sound of gunfire to the west meant that German columns had slipped past the American positions and cut them off.

Throughout the night and into the next day the unequal struggle for Longvilly continued. This was another of those "hold at any cost" positions, and the cost was high. Finally there was nothing left but to retreat. Team Cherry of the 10th Armored tried valiantly to open an escape route, but guns from all three German divisions zeroed in on the retreating column choking the single road and tore it apart. Quickly the road became a long, narrow inferno of flame and smoke, fed by the smashed gas tanks of some 200 American vehicles. The focus of destruction was a roadside shrine, where scores of wrecked, fire-blackened trucks, jeeps, tanks, self-propelled guns, and armored cars—and the bodies of the men who had manned them—lay strewn among the stone crucifixes and the serene statues of religious figures.

One of the Nazi columns that had slipped past the American roadblock at Longvilly during the night was the spearhead of Panzer Lehr, led by the division commander himself, Major General Fritz Bayerlein. Earlier in the war, Bayerlein had served in North Africa under the bold and daring Erwin Rommel, the "Desert Fox"; now, just a few miles from Bastogne, Bayerlein decided on the sort of quick thrust that had made his former commander famous.

With fifteen tanks and four companies of assault infantry in halftracks, he abandoned the paved highway he was on and turned down a secondary road that led straight toward Bastogne. As the column crawled through the darkness, the road became narrower and narrower until it was little more than a muddy cow path. In the early hours of December 19 the Germans reached the village of Mageret, barely three miles from Bastogne. There Bayerlein questioned a Belgian civilian, who imaginatively described "a very great force" of ninety American tanks and armored cars that had just passed through the village; this was in fact Team Cherry's thirty tanks sent to help out at Longvilly.

At that moment Bastogne was Bayerlein's for the taking: virtually all the American armor was well to the east or the north, manning road-blocks; the paratroopers of the 101st Airborne were straggling into their bivouac west of the town, exhausted and disorganized and far from ready for battle. Bayerlein, however, was suddenly overcome by caution. He was, after all, no Rommel. It was dark and foggy and the road was poor, there was a good deal of firing behind him, and he was worried that the "very great force" the Belgian had described was about to close in on him from the rear. He decided to stay where he was and think again about taking Bastogne when daylight came.

Taking Bastogne in the daylight hours of December 19 was going to be considerably more difficult than taking it a few hours before might have been. At Noville, north of Bastogne, the 2nd Panzer collided with one of Roberts' 10th Armored teams. Bayerlein's Panzer Lehr, rolling forward confidently, ran squarely into a regiment of 101st Division paratroopers led by Lieutenant Colonel Julian Ewell. Ewell had pushed swiftly through Bastogne in the early morning hours, and his boldness paid off: Bayerlein was stopped cold.

That morning the Germans also met another of those pesky First Army engineers who had made life so miserable for Kampfgruppe Peiper at Trois Ponts and at Werbomont the day before. Private Bernard Michin, a tall, gawky young engineer from Rhode Island, had never fired a bazooka in his life, but at dawn on December 19 he was crouching nervously in a roadside ditch near the village of Neffe armed with one.

In the foggy half-light he heard the squeaking clatter of tank tracks. The range of a bazooka was about 150 yards, but Michin was not too sure of what he was doing and he worried about hitting an American tank by mistake. So he waited until he was positive it was German before he fired—at a range of ten yards. The bazooka rocket sliced into the big Tiger and blew it up with a roar, blocking the rest of a panzer column strung out behind it.

Michin saw none of this. He didn't know that a bazookaman was supposed to wear special dark glasses, and the flash of the bazooka and the bigger flash of the exploding tank seared his eyes and temporarily blinded him. As he tumbled into the bottom of the ditch, a German machine gun opened up at him. "I got kinda nervous," he later explained; guided only by sound, he hurled a hand grenade, smashing the machine gun and killing its crew. Eight hours later, at an aid station, he recovered his sight.

By now the rest of the 11,000 Screaming Eagles of the 101st Airborne were joining the 10th Armored in the defensive perimeter around Bastogne, and German progress became painfully slow. A heavy fog kept lifting and descending like a theater curtain; whenever it lifted, the Germans were caught in the open and subjected to a withering fire.

The scene in Bastogne itself was hectic. German shells were shrieking into the town and there were stragglers everywhere, plodding dejectedly toward the rear as the jeering paratroopers passed them on their way to the front. In Middleton's command post the situation map had an ominous look. There were far more of the red-crayon symbols for the enemy than the blue markings for U.S. units; "It looks like it's got the measles," remarked one of the airborne officers.

On General Bradley's orders, Middleton pulled his headquarters out of Bastogne to a spot where he could better command the fighting, leaving the defense of the town to the

101st's McAuliffe. Forty-six-year-old Tony McAuliffe was an artillery specialist, a short, stocky man of few words and strong opinions. Commanding with him was Colonel Roberts of CCB, 10th Armored, a hard-bitten veteran who had fought in World War I and whose opinions were as strong as McAuliffe's.

These two tough-minded soldiers soon would form an effective team, but it took some doing. The problem was that the paratroopers seldom had fought alongside tanks, and it was their idea that armor should be parked right up with them on the firing line, like steel pillboxes. Roberts would have none of that: tanks, he insisted, were for mobile fighting, and must be kept grouped for hard-hitting counterattacks. Once the two men had educated each other, they got along fine.

In addition to Roberts' tanks, McAuliffe's ace in the hole was his artillery: the guns of his own division, those he inherited from Middleton, and some stragglers, such as a battery of powerful 155-mm. "Long Toms" whose Negro gunners drifted in from the battle to the east and stayed to fight. Another welcome addition was a battalion of tank destroyers that had made its perilous way southward across the battlefield to Bastogne a hop, skip, and jump ahead of the enemy. Finally, there was a mixed bag of stragglers blown loose from their units—riflemen, cooks, truck drivers, and the like—collected into Team Snafu (army slang for "Situation Normal, All Fouled Up") to guard the Bastogne command post. All in all, the garrison was the equivalent of about a division and a half. It was outnumbered by three or four to one.

By December 20 the German high command was more than a little impatient at the delay in taking Bastogne, and sharp orders came down to the local corps commander, Lieutenant General Heinrich von Lüttwitz, to get on with it. Lüttwitz first decided to get rid of the annoyingly stubborn CCB team in Noville, five miles north of Bastogne, that was blocking the 2nd Panzer's westward drive. By noon the fog-shrouded town was surrounded. Aided by paratroopers, the tankers fought their way through the ring with heavy losses, but the Germans were too spent to follow up the victory.

At the same time, McAuliffe was getting alarming reports from Marvie, a village two miles southeast of Bastogne, where Panzer Lehr was trying a quick, hard thrust with armor and half-tracks full of infantry.

The panzers made short work of a handful of U.S. light tanks in Marvie and charged recklessly into the village with guns blazing. A pair of Sherman tanks caught them from the flank and knocked out two. From their foxholes paratroopers fired at the half-tracks and in turn were cut down by machine guns. Bazookamen met the remaining panzers head-on in the main street and smashed them, the last one going up like a torch under fire from three sides. For two hours there was vicious house-to-house fighting until the last German was killed or captured.

Still Lüttwitz was not through. That evening crack panzergrenadiers, supported by tanks and assault guns, attacked from the east on a wide front. Their morale was high and they came on shouting, but artilleryman McAuliffe had carefully ranged in his guns and he laid down a terrible "dam of fire" right on top of them. U.S. tank destroyers dueled with the panzers, each firing at the other's gun flashes. As the grenadiers kept coming, the machine guns and rifles and mortars of the dug-in paratroopers added to the din. Tracer bullets streaked redly across the open fields like an uncountable shower of meteors. In the darkness a great mass of Germans stumbled headlong into a checkerboard of barbed wire fencing that Belgian farmers used for penning cattle. Trapped in the wire, they were mowed down by the score, their bodies piling up three and four deep.

At midnight the firing at last sputtered out, and the ghastly battlefield was silent except for the moaning of the wounded. North, south, and east, the Bastogne perimeter had held.

While Lüttwitz was trying to batter his way into Bastogne, fast-moving German columns kept driving westward on either side of the town. By December 21 they had completely ringed it. Bastogne was now an island in a hostile sea.

Unlike regular infantrymen, paratroopers were trained to fight behind enemy lines, and they took in stride the news that they were surrounded. "The cutting of the roads," a Screaming Eagle wryly noted in a situation report, "had no effect upon our present situation except to make travel hazardous."

For the moment the Battle of Bastogne was a stand-off. General Manteuffel was in a quandary. His Fifth Panzer Army was supposed to drive to the Meuse, take Bastogne, and guard the left flank until the slow-moving Seventh Army could catch up, and he simply did not yet have the strength to do all three jobs at the same time. With both St. Vith and Bastogne still in American hands, the road network available to him was too limited to bring up reinforcements or even to supply the divisions that he had in the field.

The Germans could not get into Bastogne, and the Americans could not strike out at them either. McAuliffe's chief worries were his wounded and his ammunition stocks. The 101st's hospital unit had been ambushed, and he was woefully short of medical supplies and doctors to treat the wounded overflowing the aid stations. To add to his troubles, the weather now turned icy cold and it began to snow. With a great many Germans between Bastogne and Patton's Third Army coming up from the south, and with the weather too bad for aerial resupply, McAuliffe had to ration his precious artillery to ten rounds a day per gun.

Bastogne's 3,500 civilians had been forced underground into dank, cold, dimly lit cellars to escape the constant German shelling, yet they showed no signs of panic. Young Renée Lemaire, the pretty daughter of the local hardware merchant, volunteered to nurse the wounded, and everyone cheerfully donated white linens and sheets to camouflage the American emplacements when it began to snow. "For four or five days we lived in a sort of dream," Mayor Léon Jacqmin recalled. "There was just one agonizing question: would the Germans succeed in taking the town?"

So far frustrated at every turn, General Lüttwitz now tried a new tactic. At 11:30 on the morning of December 22 an American outpost reported that four Germans were walking toward them carrying a white bedspread on a pole as a flag of truce. The news flashed from foxhole to foxhole; typically, the cocky paratroopers concluded that the besieging Nazi army had had enough and wanted to surrender.

It was, of course, just the opposite. The Germans carried a note addressed to "the U.S.A. Commander." "There is only one possibility of saving the encircled U.S.A. troops from total annihilation: the honorable surrender of the encircled town," it read. It went on to say that an entire corps of artillery—this was pure invention on Lüttwitz' part—would demolish Bastogne if the surrender demand was rejected. "All the serious civilian losses caused by this artillery fire would not correspond with the well-known American humanity," it piously concluded.

The note was taken to the Bastogne command post and given to Chief of Staff Ned Moore. "What's on the paper, Ned?" General McAuliffe asked.

"They want us to surrender."

McAuliffe glanced at the note. "Aw, nuts!" he said with a laugh and tossed it on the floor.

On second thought, however, McAuliffe realized that the note was a formal military communication that required some sort of answer from him.

"What the hell should I tell them?" he asked his staff.

"That first remark of yours would be hard to beat, General," Lieutenant Colonel Harry Kinnard, the operations officer, suggested.

"What'd I say?" McAuliffe asked, puzzled.

"You said, 'Nuts!'"

Everyone in the command post agreed that this would be beautifully appropriate. McAuliffe sat down with pen and paper and quickly dashed off his reply:

TO THE GERMAN COMMANDER:

NUTS!

THE AMERICAN COMMANDER

"Will you see that it's delivered?" he asked Colonel Joe Harper, commander of the sector in which the German envoys were being held. Like everyone else in the room, Harper had a big grin on his face. "I'll deliver it myself. It will be a lot of fun."

At his command post Harper handed the reply to the German major who had brought the surrender demand. The major, a particularly arrogant type, did not know what to make of it. "Is that reply negative or affirmative?" he asked stiffly. "If it is the latter I will negotiate further."

Harper lost his temper. "If you don't understand what 'Nuts' means, in plain English it's the same as 'Go to Hell!' And I'll tell you something else. If you continue to attack we'll kill every goddam German that tries to break into this city!" The major snapped off a salute and returned to his lines. The threatened artillery barrage never came.

The whole episode had a comic-opera quality about it, and "Nuts" was the perfect barb to explode the bluff. Manteuffel was infuriated when he learned about it. He considered the surrender demand an insult to German military honor, a confession of weakness that was sure to raise American morale. Lüttwitz became a laughingstock throughout the army and never lived it down.

The Battle of the Bulge was now a week old, and so far the miserable weather conditions were everything the Germans could ask for. Thick clouds and fog had effectively prevented Allied planes from taking a hand in the fighting. But December 23 dawned cold and clear, and American hopes rose all through the Ardennes —nowhere higher than in Bastogne.

At 9:30 A.M. a C-47 transport plane appeared over the town and a team of pathfinders parachuted into the perimeter. They set up radar sets and brightly colored cloth panels to guide a great fleet of transports on the way from England. By noon the crisp blue sky over Bastogne was filled with silver planes, spilling out supply bundles under vivid red, blue, green, and yellow parachutes. German anti-aircraft fire knocked down several of the C-47's, but the pilots of the rest never wavered. GI's collected containers of ammunition, food, clothing, blood plasma for the wounded, and gasoline for CCB's tanks. Fully ninety-five per cent of the 144 tons of supplies landed safely within the perimeter. "A tribute is an awkward thing," wrote paratrooper Captain Laurence Critchell. "Even the men who felt like waving their arms and yelling did nothing at all except stare up in silence at the roaring planes."

When U.S. Thunderbolts flying cover for the C-47's had shepherded their charges safely away, they came back to work over the German positions encircling Bastogne. Captain Critchell watched admiringly:

"The planes dive on some object behind the German positions, then pull up in a fine curve a few hundred feet off the ground, leaving behind, where the bomb struck, a perfectly formed balloon of orange flame and black smoke which expanded soundlessly, brilliantly, and with spectacular beauty over the dazzling, snow-white hills. Moments later the sound would come...."

In the next few days, when weather permitted, the Air Force delivered almost a thousand more tons of supplies to Bastogne, and Allied fighters bombed and strafed the German positions. All this forced General Lüttwitz to redouble his efforts to take Bastogne before it became too strong to take at all.

At dusk on December 23 the Germans struck a second time at Marvie, where the American perimeter ran closest to Bastogne. Enemy infantry in white uniforms crept through the snow undetected and surrounded a platoon of ninety-eight GI's on a commanding hill near the village. Four tanks charged up the hill, and radio communications with the platoon went out. The defenders were never heard from again.

An American half-track fleeing from this attack raced into the streets of Marvie, where paratroopers, thinking it was a captured vehicle leading the enemy charge, blasted it into a flaming wreck, killing the entire crew. Ironically, this tragic error helped to save Marvie. When German tanks came slashing into the village, they found the wrecked half-track completely blocking the main street. Bazooka fire ripped into them as they tried to turn around. A bitter fire fight raged among Marvie's burning houses until two of Colonel Roberts' Shermans arrived to help drive the Germans back.

Just to the west a second panzer column tried to smash its way through a roadblock barely a mile from Bastogne. Firing bazookas from their foxholes, the paratroopers blunted the thrust at a range of only fifty yards. "We were stopped before we could begin," General Bayerlein complained. Two panzers did manage to slip through and drive all the way into Bastogne. After shooting up buildings around McAuliffe's command post, they were disposed of by Team Snafu.

Stymied again at Marvie, Lüttwitz licked his wounds and scheduled an all-out attack for

December 25. In the meantime the Luftwaffe made Christmas Eve miserable for the defenders of Bastogne. Two waves of bombers plastered the town during the night, setting many buildings on fire and wrecking CCB's command post, killing four of its officers. A direct hit on an aid station killed twenty wounded GI's and young Renée Lemaire, their volunteer Belgian nurse.

This bombing had a particularly depressing effect on the Bastogne garrison. On Christmas Day the paratroopers huddled in their frozen foxholes, their feet wrapped in burlap bags, munching K rations and gloomily speculating on whether they would ever see another Christmas. Fifteen miles away, General Hasso von Manteuffel also was eating a Christmas dinner of American K rations, musing on the fact that exactly one year before he had enjoyed a magnificent Christmas feast as the guest of Adolf Hitler.

For his Christmas Day attack General Lüttwitz chose an untested sector of the American perimeter: the village of Champs, northwest of Bastogne. At dawn a powerful force of tanks and assault infantry from a fresh division sprang forward.

An American outpost telephoned a frantic warning to Colonel Ray Allen at battalion headquarters: "Tanks are coming toward you!" Allen asked how close they were. "If you look out your window now you'll be looking right down the muzzle of an 88," came the reply. Glancing out the window, Allen agreed with the estimate. As shells hit the command post, he and his staff fled for the cover of nearby woods. Glancing back, Allen saw the German tank firing at him. He was running as fast as he could, but the German gunner was overestimating his speed and leading him too much. Allen dived gratefully into the cover of the trees.

The line of paratroopers defending Champs was thin, and a column of eighteen white-painted Mark IV tanks, carrying grenadiers on their decks, burst through it with a rush. In the crisis, cooks, clerks, headquarters staff, and anyone else who had a gun were sent rushing to head them off. A doctor combed his aid station for every man who could walk, gave each a rifle, and sent them hobbling into the fight.

This was to be the finest hour for Bastogne's tank destroyer battalion. Sergeant Lawrence Valletta maneuvered his TD through the streets of Champs, literally blowing German infantry out of every house they tried to find cover in. Two other well-concealed tank destroyers ambushed a company of the Mark IV's that had broken through, knocking out three in rapid succession. Bazookas accounted for two more, artillery got another, and the seventh and last was captured intact when it stalled.

The other company of Mark IV's unwittingly drove straight into a murderous cross fire from tanks, tank destroyers, artillery, and bazookas. "The German tanks were fired at from so many directions and with such a mixture of fire that it was not possible to see or say how each tank

met its doom," concluded a historian of the
action. "Eighteen tanks had driven on through
the infantry," he noted. "Not one got away."

With its armored heart cut out, the assault
on Champs slowly dwindled away. That night
a "last desperate effort," as the German commander described it, was cut to ribbons by the
deadly American artillery. The battle of Christmas Day was over. A sense of confidence,
almost of invincibility, now infected the Bastogne garrison. They had met and stopped the
best the German had; Bastogne, they were sure,
would never be taken.

Shortly after noon on December 26 Lieutenant Colonel Creighton Abrams halted his Sherman tank at a crossroads five miles south of
Bastogne. Abrams' twenty Shermans were the
spearhead of the 4th Armored Division of Patton's Third Army, and for four days they had
been pounding northward against stubborn
German resistance. Patton had promised to be
in Bastogne by Christmas, and already he was
a day behind schedule. Abrams radioed for
permission to gamble on one hard, fast punch
straight toward the town. Patton agreed. Stick-
ing a big cigar in his mouth, Abrams snapped
out his orders: "We're going in to those people
now. Let 'er roll!"

Trailed by half-tracks full of infantry, the
Shermans took off at top speed. At a small village they were stopped by a roadblock supported by a pair of deadly German 88's. Nineteen-
year-old Private Jimmy Hendrix leaped out of
a half-track, killed two Germans manning the

roadblock, and ran straight at the 88's, howling like an Indian and waving his rifle. The scared German gunners stood up, hands raised in surrender. The tanks rolled forward again, spraying the woods on each side of the road with their machine guns.

At 4:30 that afternoon, Tuesday, December 26, Lieutenant Charles Boggess in the lead tank saw a line of foxholes up ahead. According to his map, he ought to be near the Bastogne perimeter. "Come on out," he shouted. There was no response. "It's all right, it's the 4th Armored." Cautiously a figure climbed out of a foxhole, carefully looked the Sherman over, and then hurried forward.

"I'm Lieutenant Webster of the 326th Engineers, 101st Airborne," he said to Boggess, grinning broadly and shaking hands. "Glad to see you!"

Thus the German stranglehold on Bastogne was broken. Very heavy fighting would continue around the town for more than two weeks, but the immediate crisis was over. The battle had lasted nine days and it had cost the Bastogne defenders between 2,500 and 3,500 casualties (in the confused early days no accurate count was possible). It had cost the Germans far more than they could afford to pay—in men, in time, in strategic position.

Patton's men were welcomed warmly enough by the garrison, but Tony McAuliffe and his Battered Bastards of Bastogne would always insist that they had not been rescued. Helped, perhaps; but they had never needed rescuing.

V

CLIMAX AT THE MEUSE

British Field Marshal Bernard Montgomery was a small and rather bird-like man of careful habits, who liked his battles to be as precise and tidy as he was himself. The battle he inherited in the northern half of the Ardennes on December 20, however, was as untidy as a battle could possibly be.

All along the northern rim of the German breakthrough First Army GI's under Courtney Hodges were struggling desperately to contain the enemy's thrusts. Means of communication, chains of command, and lines of supply were broken and tangled; the defenses-in-depth and tactical reserves so dear to military textbook writers hardly existed. The single common element was a sullen, stubborn determination to make the Nazis pay in blood for every foot of ground they gained.

In Bernard Montgomery's view, the way to tidy up this northern battlefield was to hold at all costs the shoulder of the Bulge at Elsenborn Ridge so that the Germans could not widen the breach; to straighten Hodges' patchwork line by "voluntary withdrawals"; to let the Germans spend themselves driving westward with ever-lengthening supply lines; and finally, with a carefully assembled reserve force, to smash the tip of the salient with a carefully timed assault. It was all very precise, very neat, very scientific.

As the Field Marshal soon discovered when he sought to withdraw the U.S. units defending St. Vith (see Chapter 3), his American allies did not entirely share his views. "Once they had recovered from the first shock, the American troops were out for vengeance," wrote British historian Chester Wilmot. "Having suffered the ignominy of surprise and defeat, their instinctive reaction was to hold fast to whatever they were still holding and to strike back wherever they could as soon and as hard as possible."

The overriding strategic philosophy of the United States Army was aggressive attack. American officers had been trained under that old military maxim, "The best defense is a good offense." General Omar Bradley, for example, never had fought a defensive action before the Battle of the Bulge—and never had to fight one afterward. What Montgomery had on his hands, then, was a group of very aggressive-minded

American generals whose ideas often were very different from his own.

Nevertheless, Montgomery moved energetically to flesh out his plan and bring order to the tangled battlefield. He hurried light British forces to the west bank of the Meuse to guard the all-important bridges spanning the river. British armor and infantry were ordered into position northwest of the Meuse to strike any German columns that might cross the river and threaten Brussels and Antwerp. Most important, he began putting together a reserve force for a counterattack.

To lead this reserve, Montgomery chose Major General J. Lawton "Lightning Joe" Collins, the fast-moving commander of Hodges' VII Corps. Since most of Collins' troops already were committed to the battle, the Allied high command had to reach far and wide to create a reserve: the 3rd Armored Division from his old command, the 2nd Armored and 84th Infantry divisions from the U.S. Ninth Army to the north, and the 75th Infantry Division, newly arrived from the United States. Collins was ordered to mass this four-division striking force in the northwest corner of the Ardennes—and to avoid all contact with the enemy until Montgomery decided it was time to unleash it.

All these moves looked fine on paper. On the battlefield, however, the opponent always has something to say about a general's best-laid plans; and Montgomery's opponent, Field Marshal Model, had no intention whatever of

Once the German grip on Bastogne was broken, supply convoys poured into the snowy streets of the town. This picture was taken in January, 1945, during the U.S. drive to reduce the Bulge.

The premier weapon in the American defense of Elsenborn Ridge, at the northern edge of the German breakthrough, was the artillery. This 155-mm. howitzer is hidden from Luftwaffe spotter planes by camouflage netting.

British Field Marshal Bernard Montgomery (center) stands with two of his field commanders after taking charge of the northern half of the battlefield. At left, Major General J. Lawton Collins of the VII Corps; at right, Major General Matthew Ridgway of the XVIII Corps. The German attack split General Bradley's 12th Army Group in half, with the First Army in the north and the Third Army in the south. Believing it would be difficult, if not impossible, for Bradley to communicate with the two armies, General Eisenhower informed Bradley that he was giving temporary command of all the American troops on the north side of the salient to Montgomery. Eisenhower's action infuriated Bradley.

GI's from the 7th Armored Division man an antitank gun sited to fire down the main street of a hamlet near the town of Vielsalm. Survivors of the fight for St. Vith withdrew through this area on December 23, the date that this picture was taken.

Covered by the rifleman at the right, First Army engineers prepare demolition charges on a railroad trestle at Vielsalm. These troops, like the gunners in the previous photograph (both pictures were taken the same day), are guarding a withdrawal route from the so-called Goose Egg.

The American defenders of Hotton inspect two of their victims, a self-propelled gun (at left) and a Panther tank. The plate over the Panther's treads was for protection against bazooka fire.

This is Manhay, or what was left of it after the bitter seesaw fight for control of its road network. This American jeep was one of the several wrecked vehicles.

Part of the array of 2nd Panzer Division weapons and vehicles captured in the Battle of Celles, photographed at a U.S. assembly point. Many vehicles, their gas tanks empty, were seized intact. At the right are antitank guns; beyond them is a Panther tank.

Infantrymen from one of "Lightning Joe" Collins' divisions, the 84th, hastily dig in under the fire of German artillery that has just killed the man in the foreground.

The Germans turned this barn along the northern edge of the Bulge into a strongpoint. To the right, two GI's of the 7th Armored Division advance past a smouldering Nazi tank destroyer.

A pair of American Thunderbolt fighter-bombers take off on a mission. This was one of the airfields hit by the Luftwaffe in its surprise attack on New Year's Day.

On January 16, 1945, such meetings as this one, between a crewman of a Third Army armored car and two First Army GI's, symbolized the successful reduction of the Bulge.

This German prisoner was taken in the last days of the Battle of the Bulge. He was from one of the ill-trained divisions that the Nazis had raised hurriedly from their last reserves of manpower for the offensive.

As the Third Reich collapsed in Spring 1945, Allied prisoner-of-war camps like this one overflowed. In the Ruhr Field Marshal Walther Model committed suicide rather than join his 325,000 troops in surrender.

Belgian refugees move their pitiful belongings out of the path of the counterattacking U.S. First Army. It is inevitable that on any battlefield, whatever the outcome, the civilians will be the losers.

The American infantryman met and passed his ultimate test in the Battle of the Bulge. "Without orders or information," wrote a historian in tribute, these GI's "simply took things in their own hands and fought back."

presenting the Allies with a gift of time to pull themselves together and regain the initiative.

As Montgomery developed his strategy, the Nazi high command was studying its situation maps with a mixture of satisfaction and frustration. On the credit side was the fact that the 2nd Panzer Division of Manteuffel's army finally had sidestepped Bastogne and grabbed the key bridge at Ortheuville in the central Ardennes, putting the spearhead of Operation Christrose across the barrier of the Ourthe River, thirty miles from the Meuse. Coming up fast in support was the crack 116th Panzer, the Greyhound Division, fresh from capturing 25,000 precious gallons of gasoline at an American fuel depot. By December 21, St. Vith had been taken and Bastogne was encircled. And morale in the ranks was still high. On December 22, in a letter home, a German lieutenant named Rockhammer wrote: "Our soldiers still have the old zip. Always advancing and smashing everything. The snow must turn red with American blood. Victory was never so close as it is now. We will throw them into the ocean...."

The high command's frustration was centered on Sepp Dietrich's Sixth Panzer Army. Dietrich still was stymied by the Americans on Elsenborn Ridge, who were shelling his SS troops unmercifully. His advance guard, Kampfgruppe Peiper, was in grave danger at Stoumont, cut off when the Americans recaptured Stavelot, nine miles behind it. Supply columns sent to Peiper's aid were making little progress. In fact, because of the limited road network, German supply columns were making little progress anywhere in the Ardennes.

Hitler's original victory timetable had been knocked into a cocked hat, of course, although this did not particularly disturb the German frontline generals. They had not really expected that on this sixth day of Operation Christrose they would be across the Meuse and driving toward Antwerp; they knew it would never be *that* easy.

Kampfgruppe Peiper might be trapped, but it was still as dangerous as a wounded tiger. Its key strongpoint was the St. Edouard tuberculosis sanatorium at Stoumont, a large, stone fortresslike building on a height overlooking the village. Peiper's men were dug in inside and around the sanatorium, strongly supported by tanks and artillery. Huddled in the cellar were 200 sick children and old people, cared for by Catholic priests and nursing nuns.

On the evening of December 20, under cover of a heavy fog, three companies from the U.S. 30th Division had seized the sanatorium in a surprise assault. But a few hours later counterattacking Germans swarmed back into the building, driving the GI's out room by room, capturing thirty-two of them, and knocking out their supporting Shermans with bazookas.

For two more days the bloody fight for Stoumont continued without pause. Attacking Shermans, outgunned by their rival Panthers and Tigers, were knocked out or driven back. American tank destroyers and heavy artillery, however, pounded the sanatorium with deadly accuracy, their fire directed by a squad of GI's hidden in a nearby outbuilding. In the cellar the priests and nuns tried to calm the terrified children as walls and roof beams crashed down above them and smoke and debris filled the room. One heavy shell penetrated halfway through the cellar ceiling—and failed to explode.

On December 22, U.S. engineers finished hacking a road through the thick forest on a ridge behind the sanatorium and tanks began to pour a murderous fire into the rear of the building. This was too much for Peiper's men, and they pulled out. GI's carried the tearful children to safety through the heaped rubble. Miraculously, not a single one of them had been hurt. Father Hanlet paused to kneel in the shattered chapel amid the bodies of American and German soldiers. "God, who has saved us, welcome in Your mercy the fallen fighters of this place," he prayed.

Joachim Peiper at last admitted defeat. Completely out of fuel and nearly out of ammunition, he set fire to his remaining vehicles and led 800 survivors on a perilous night march through the encircling American lines. Behind him he left the smouldering hulks of 28 tanks, 70 half-tracks, and 25 pieces of artillery. Kampfgruppe Peiper, which had set out so confidently for the Meuse on December 17, was no more.

While Peiper and his men made their last fight, the front to the east erupted like a volcano. Sepp Dietrich was throwing everything he had against Elsenborn Ridge in a determined effort to get his Sixth Panzer Army moving.

Elsenborn Ridge is an L-shaped piece of high ground that comes down from the north behind the twin villages of Krinkelt and Rocherath and then angles westward. At the point of the angle is the tiny hamlet of Dom Butgenbach; there, dug in behind barbed wire and logs and sand-bags and with artillery to back it up, was the 2nd Battalion, 26th Regiment, U.S. 1st Infantry Division—the famous "Big Red One" division that claimed for itself first place in the entire United States Army.

Beginning before dawn on December 19, and lasting ninety-six hours, Lieutenant Colonel Derrill Daniel's 2nd Battalion endured an ordeal unmatched by any American unit in the Battle of the Bulge. Six separate assaults, made under cover of darkness and fog, were driven against the battalion by some of the hardest-fighting troops in Dietrich's army. Six times Daniel's men threw them back.

The American artillery was instrumental in beating off the first two attacks on the 19th. At 6 A.M. on the 20th, twenty tanks and a bat-talion of riflemen hit Dom Butgenbach from two directions. GI's in foxholes shot down most of the infantry, but several tanks broke through into the village. Anti-tank guns around the battalion command post fired point-blank at the flickering engine exhausts of the Panthers in the darkness and knocked out two of them. The rest fled. Two hours later more panzers broke through, to be stopped this time by bazooka fire. When one of the German tank commanders incautiously stuck his head out of his turret, Corporal Henry Warner shot him down with a .45- caliber pistol. Warner was to be one of the heroes of the Dom Butgenbach battle, personally accounting for three German tanks before he was killed stalking a fourth.

The strongest of the six assaults was launched on December 21. For three hours German artillery and rocket batteries blasted the American lines. As dawn was breaking, a spearhead of a dozen panzers ripped through a half-mile gap torn in the 2nd Battalion, machine-gunning scores of GI's who tried to stop them with rifles and grenades. Here, it seemed, was the breakthrough that Sepp Dietrich had been looking for.

But like old-time cavalry coming to the rescue of a besieged wagon train, a unit of U.S. tank destroyers appeared at the critical moment. These TD's were a new type that mounted a powerful 90-mm. gun; one of them polished off no less than seven Panthers in a row that briefly silhouetted themselves against the dawn light as they tried to cross a ridge line. A pair of Shermans accounted for two more before they themselves were knocked out. The last of the Panthers scrambled for cover among the buildings of Dom Butgenbach, but by noon the tank destroyers had hunted them all down. Gunners on the surrounding hills fired 10,000 rounds in eight hours to all but wipe out the mass of German infantry supporting the attack, putting the final seal on the break-through.

The savage four-day battle cost Daniel's battalion very heavy casualties, but it could claim a major role in the successful defense of Elsenborn Ridge. The Sixth Panzer Army never fully recovered from its failure to break the American grip on this vital piece of landscape.

The American front that stretched west from Elsenborn Ridge, under the command of Major General Matthew Ridgway, was a prime example of the untidiness that upset Field Marshal Montgomery. It ran from Malmédy to the Ourthe River, halfway through the Ardennes, a distance as the crow flies of thirty miles. But there were so many twists and turns and loops in it that Ridgway's XVIII Corps was actually defending a front of nearly a hundred miles.

Matt Ridgway, trained as an airborne officer, was one of those generals who gloried in solving difficult problems. On December 22, he had all the problems he could possibly want. The biggest one was called the Goose Egg.

The American troops driven from St. Vith the night before had taken refuge in the hilly, broken country west of the town in an egg-shaped salient that was precariously attached to the rest of the U.S. front at the town of Vielsalm. Montgomery wanted the Goose Egg evacuated. Ridgway urged that it be held as a starting point for a counterattack to recapture St. Vith. At the Vielsalm headquarters of Bob Hasbrouck, commander of the 7th Armored Division that had defended St. Vith, Ridgway outlined his plan.

"What do you think of making a stand inside

this area?" he asked Hasbrouck. "You'd hold out until a counteroffensive caught up with you. You'll soon be surrounded, of course, but we'll supply you by air."

For five days the 7th Armored had battled to the very limits of endurance in St. Vith. Hasbrouck knew that his remaining tanks were in bad shape and that his tankers were exhausted, half-frozen, and fought-out. "I don't like it," he said. "My people are only fifty percent effective. And I'm sure that goes for the infantry."

Unconvinced, Ridgway toured the Goose Egg to question the various unit commanders. Their answers were the same: one more hard attack and the Goose Egg would crack wide open. Late that afternoon he returned to Hasbrouck's headquarters, disappointed but at last convinced.

"Bob, start pulling your people back as soon as possible," he ordered. "I want them all withdrawn under cover of darkness tonight."

Hasbrouck and his staff immediately set to work planning the withdrawal. It was a staggering task. There were some 22,000 men from a half-dozen different outfits in the Goose Egg. Their vehicles were in poor condition, the few roads were narrow and deep in slush and mud, and the whole force would have to pull back across the Salm River through a corridor less than two miles wide around Vielsalm. The withdrawal was timed to start at 2 A.M. on the 23rd, but by that hour not all the units had received their orders. Others that had were riveted in place by the pressure of fierce German attacks. If the men in the Goose Egg were going to pull out, they would have to do it in broad daylight.

The miserable condition of the roads worried Hasbrouck as much as anything else. Then, in the hours just before dawn on December 23, a harsh, frigid wind began to blow across the Ardennes. This was a "Russian High," a cold weather front that had drifted westward across Europe from the Russian plains. In their foxholes GI's grumbled and huddled deeper into their overcoats—those who were lucky enough to have them. Few guessed that the bitter cold was going to save many of their lives. By dawn the rutted, muddy roads in the Goose Egg had frozen solid.

Quickly detachments began to "peel off" and head west toward the Vielsalm bridges, protected by rear guards of armor. German shelling grew heavy as panzers and infantry probed the thinning perimeter. One American column was halted briefly when enemy anti-tank guns knocked out its lead tanks; thanks to the Russian High, the rest of the column was able to edge around the burning Shermans through a frozen field. Another German assault on one of the escape routes was broken up by Lightning and Thunderbolt fighter-bombers, finding good hunting as the skies over the Ardennes cleared at last.

At Vielsalm, General Hasbrouck watched his columns rumble steadily across the bridges, the men packed into trucks and half-tracks and clinging to the decks of the armored vehicles, tired, unshaven, filthy, and cold—but safe. By evening the evacuation of the Goose Egg was complete. Bob Hasbrouck had pulled off one of war's most difficult feats—a withdrawal from an exposed position in daylight under enemy fire. Adding that accomplishment to his brilliant defense of St. Vith, it is easy to see why historian Wilmot called him "one of the great men of the Ardennes."

The battle was sliding steadily westward as Model tried to turn the flank of Hodges' First Army—and in the process raised havoc with Montgomery's plan to build up a reserve for a counterattack. As early as December 21, as the fight for St. Vith reached its climax, a German armored column appeared out of nowhere at the village of Hotton, twenty-five miles to the west. The U.S. 3rd Armored Division, earmarked for Lightning Joe Collins' counterattack, finally managed to contain this new threat. In the struggle, however, one of its task forces was cut off and surrounded.

Lieutenant Colonel Sam Hogan, the task force commander, was ambushed but managed to escape on foot and rejoin his unit the next day. For four more days "Hogan's 400" held out. On Christmas Eve the Germans demanded their surrender. "We have orders to fight to the death," Hogan told the German officer carrying a flag of truce. "Tell your commander to go to hell." This was not quite so dramatic as Tony McAuliffe's remark in besieged Bastogne, but the meaning was just as clear. Task Force

Hogan finally ran out of supplies, disabled its vehicles, and walked out, losing just one man.

By December 23, despite Montgomery's orders to stay clear of the fight and prepare for a counterattack in ten days or so, two more of Collins' divisions were sucked into the spreading fight along the northern flank. Everywhere they looked Collins and Ridgway had a crisis on their hands. Even as the Goose Egg was being evacuated, a fresh German armored division lashed out suddenly and captured a roadblock eight miles to the west on the important highway N-15 that led northward toward the great American supply center of Liège.

(This new division was the 2nd SS Panzer, whose appearance caused much confusion among American Intelligence officers trying to keep track of the enemy's "order of battle." There were just too many 2nd divisions on the battlefield: on highway N-15 was the 2nd SS Panzer, one of the elite formations in Hitler's "private army"; to the west was the German regular army's 2nd Panzer Division, leading Manteuffel's drive to the Meuse; and to confuse matters further, the 2nd Panzer was just then tangling with patrols from its American opposite number, the 2nd Armored Division from Collins' corps.)

By the end of Saturday, December 23, the Battle of the Bulge was eight days old. The Bulge was now forty-five miles wide and some sixty miles deep, with its tip barely four miles from the Meuse. Operation Christrose had been slowed down considerably and the break-through was too narrow to suit the Germans, but they still held the initiative.

After the collapse of the St. Vith salient and the evacuation of the Goose Egg, the American northern flank was a little closer to being tidy, yet it was far from being secure. The shoulder of the breakthrough at Elsenborn Ridge was finally rock-solid in American hands, but there were several critical areas to the west: at Man-hay, where the 2nd SS Panzer was attacking along the Liège highway; at Hotton, where the Greyhounds of the 116th Panzer threatened to break through; and at the extreme tip of the Bulge, where Manteuffel's armor had driven to within sight of the Meuse.

The southern shoulder still was firmly in American hands, thanks to the stubborn 4th Infantry Division. At Bastogne, however, the struggle was in its sixth day and the outcome remained in the balance. Patton's counterattack from the south had begun as scheduled but was meeting stiff resistance. In spite of the Bastogne bottleneck, Manteuffel (often in person) was prodding forward every man and gun and tank that he could lay his hands on to strengthen his spearhead overlooking the Meuse.

As seen by the top commanders in the field, both German and American, the Battle of the Bulge was clearly building to a climax. The next forty-eight hours would be decisive. Model and Manteuffel always had suspected that the goal of reaching Antwerp was an illu-sion. Now they were sure of it. Still, they believed that a less spectacular victory might be within their reach—a drive up the east bank of the Meuse to curl in behind the American First Army and threaten the Aachen salient that the Allies held in the Siegfried Line. Paired with a simultaneous thrust against the other side of the salient, they felt that such a strategy would inflict severe casualties on the Allies and perhaps restore Germany's shaky Western Front.

In proposing this strategy to Hitler's headquarters, the two generals warned that the Third Reich could no longer afford to keep its back turned on what was happening on the Eastern Front. German Intelligence had detected unmistakable signs that the Russians were massing for an offensive. Unless the battle in the West was stabilized soon—which meant giving up the glittering dream of crossing the Meuse—and forces released from the Ardennes to strengthen the thinned-out Eastern Front, the Russians would score a fatal breakthrough.

What seemed so clear to these commanders on the scene was not clear to Adolf Hitler. His gaze remained fixed on Christrose's promise of a sweeping victory over the Western Allies. Scorning the warnings from the East, the Führer demanded renewed efforts to cross the Meuse. At the same time, he prepared plans for a second offensive on the Western Front—not against the Aachen salient but in Alsace, south of the Ardennes. He assured his generals that this would stop Patton in his tracks and send him scurrying southward to meet the new threat.

One of the strongest reasons the German front-line generals gave for limiting the offensive was the weather. During the first week of Christrose it had been all they could ask for as a shield against Allied air power. Watching snow pelting the windows of his headquarters, Hoyt Vandenberg, commander of the U.S. Ninth Air Force, bitterly remarked, "Do you think Hitler *makes* this stuff?" But on December 23 the skies cleared at last, and Allied planes appeared over the Ardennes by the hundreds.

Heavy bombers pounded rail lines and highways and bridges east of the battlefield, choking German supply routes. Beleaguered Bastogne received its first airdrop of supplies, and elsewhere in the Ardennes anything that moved on the German-held roads attracted swarms of fighter-bombers as honey attracts flies. American Lightnings and Thunderbolts and British Typhoons, after disposing of the few Luftwaffe fighters that appeared, slashed at armored columns and supply convoys with bombs and rockets and machine guns. By nightfall, a German general recalled, every road leading into the Ardennes from the east was brightly outlined by the flames of burning vehicles.

Not all the air strikes were so well executed. That night U.S. bombers hit American-held Malmédy by mistake, killing scores of GI's and civilians. Major General Leland Hobbs, commander of the 30th Division holding Malmédy, scorched the telephone line to Ninth Air Force headquarters with a bitter tongue-lashing. Incredibly, the same mistake was repeated on the next two nights. Malmédy, reported an eyewitness, was reduced to "a burned-out pile of cinders and rubble." Dazed 30th Division GI's cursed the Ninth Air Force as the "American Luftwaffe." All told, 125 Belgian civilians and an uncounted number of American troops were killed in the three bombings. Malmédy, first the scene of massacre, now torn apart by mistake, became the blackest of names in the American memory of the Ardennes.

If the clearing cold weather was a boon to the Allied air forces, it was brutal for the infantrymen of both armies. Rain and snow already had caused an alarming increase in trench foot, and the cold made the disease worse. Cases of frostbite and exposure swelled the toll of nonbattle casualties into the thousands. In some units frostbite and trench foot took as many men out of the lines as did enemy bullets.

Private Lester Atwell, an aid man, described the foot soldier's lot that bitter December: "Their chapped hands split open, their lips cracked, their feet froze. They had heavy colds, trench foot, pneumonia, and dysentery; they became exhausted and stiff from too prolonged exposure, but they could not be relieved.... Larger and larger numbers arrived daily on sick call. After trudging several miles through deep snow or through a blizzard, in they came, their uniforms white with snow, their faces pinched, astonished, red and mottled. Even the very young looked old...."

Atwell could as well have been describing German troops as American GI's.

One of the "voluntary withdrawals" in Montgomery's scheme involved elements of the battered 7th Armored Division and the 82nd Airborne Division in the vicinity of Manhay. On December 24 they began to pull back, with "Slim Jim" Gavin grumbling that his paratroopers felt betrayed—never before had they retreated in the face of the enemy. That evening, in the midst of the withdrawal, the Germans hit Manhay with staggering force.

The Nazi armor charging up the Liège highway toward Manhay was led by a captured Sherman tank. Seeing the familiar flaring blue exhaust of the Sherman, GI's manning a roadblock assumed it was from the 7th Armored and waved the column on. Within moments the roadblock was a shambles, its defenders shot down or fleeing and four of its supporting tanks in flames. A half-mile farther on a second roadblock fell for the same ruse, and ten more Shermans were wrecked.

The American withdrawal was now close to a rout. A pair of German Tigers slipped unnoticed into one of the 7th Armored's columns; as the column ground slowly up a hill, the Tigers turned out and began to riddle the passing vehicles with their machine guns and cannon. Half-tracks and self-propelled guns slid flaming into the roadside ditches; tanks exploded under a hail of armor-piercing shells from the Tigers' 88's. What was left of the column fled cross-country in panic.

Two American tank destroyers raced up to try to block the German advance. A pair of Panthers stalked them across the dark fields. A tank destroyer got off the first shot of the duel, and one of the Panthers began to burn furiously. Its mate returned two quick rounds; the second shell sliced through the thin armor of the TD and into its ammunition rack, and it exploded with a deafening crash. The second tank destroyer opened fire, but its shell hit the heavy frontal armor of the remaining Panther and bounced off in a shower of sparks. The German's return shot hit the TD so hard that it was bowled over on its side.

The capture of Manhay by the 2nd SS Panzer not only threatened the center of Ridgway's shaky new XVIII Corps line but also dangerously exposed the great Allied supply depots of Liège, just twenty-three miles to the north. Artillery fire and the young rookies of the 75th Infantry Division (another part of Collins' reserve force), who were making their first fight, finally patched up the breach on Christmas Day.

The commitment of the 75th Division at Manhay was the last straw as far as Lightning Joe Collins was concerned. Montgomery's original timetable had called for Collins to counter-attack with four fresh divisions about January 2, 1945, but by Christmas Eve major elements of all four of these divisions already were in action from Manhay to the Meuse. The relentless German pressure was making it all but impossible to carry out the Field Marshal's wishes.

On December 24 the armored head of Manteuffel's Fifth Panzer Army lay at the village of Celles, four miles from the Meuse. American Intelligence reported that the better part of three panzer divisions were moving up to reinforce this spearhead. When they arrived, the enemy would have two choices—to drive north up the near bank of the Meuse and turn the U.S. First Army's flank (this was what Model and Manteuffel were trying to get Hitler to approve) or to vault the Meuse, either by capturing a bridge or by throwing a military span across the shallow stream. In either case, Collins knew that if the Germans were allowed to build up their strength, he would be in for a hard time.

Early on the afternoon of December 24, Field Marshal Montgomery arrived at Courtney Hodges' First Army headquarters with his solution to the problem. "Collins' situation is very critical," Montgomery said. "I very much fear we'll have to consider a general withdrawal." As he described it, Collins should swing his VII Corps back as if he were opening a door—the hinge of the door at Hotton and the outer edge touching the Meuse at the town of Andenne, well to the north.

Hodges could not believe his ears. "This will open the Meuse from Namur to Givet," he pointed out. The distance between the two towns was thirty miles.

"Don't worry, British troops will be back there," Montgomery said soothingly. "And let me say once more, I want Collins to avoid contact with the enemy as much as possible. I want Joe to keep backing off until the German has run his course." Whether the Field Marshal knew it or not, he could hardly have proposed anything more objectionable to the aggressive American commanders if he had tried.

Soon after Montgomery outlined his new plan, the first of a series of telephone calls began to come into Collins' headquarters from Major General Ernest Harmon, commander of the U.S. 2nd Armored Division. "Gravel Voice" Ernie Harmon was an outspoken, rough-hewn character; as usual, he was itching to attack. He said that his patrols had spotted the 2nd Panzer at Celles, that Belgian civilians reported the Germans were out of gas, and that now was the time to strike before the enemy was refueled and reinforced. "We've got the whole damned 2nd Panzer Division in a sack!" he roared. "You've got to give me immediate authority to attack!"

On the receiving end of this barrage was Brigadier General Williston Palmer, Collins' artillery officer. The General was away from his head-quarters, Palmer told Harmon. "You can make preliminary preparations," he added, "but you've got to wait for Joe's final decision."

By late afternoon Collins had talked to Harmon and was returning to his command post to clear the attack with higher authority, leaving Harmon fuming impatiently. He was greeted by a messenger from Hodges bearing Montgomery's new orders—or at least Hodges' carefully worded version of them.

"The VII Corps is released from all offensive missions and will go on the defensive with the objective of stabilizing the right flank of First U.S. Army," the message began. Collins, it continued, was "hereby authorized to use all forces at his disposal to accomplish the job [and] is authorized, whenever in his opinion he considers it necessary, to drop back to the general line: Andenne-Hotton."

The key word was "authorized." Hodges knew his man, knew that he would spot the loophole he had so carefully inserted in the Field Marshal's orders. Lightning Joe Collins was the man on the scene. It was up to him to decide whether to attack now or to withdraw.

It could not have surprised Hodges very much to learn that before midnight on Christmas Eve, Ernie Harmon had his orders to attack the 2nd Panzer Division at Celles the next morning.

Harmon's 2nd Armored had earned its spurs in such fierce actions as Kasserine Pass in North Africa, Anzio in Italy, and more recently, in the hard fighting at the Siegfried Line north of the Ardennes. It was well-manned and well-led, justly famous as the "Hell on Wheels" division. At 8 A.M. on Christmas Day it set out to do battle with its equally famous rival, the 2nd Panzer Division.

Having learned that the Germans were low on fuel, Harmon planned to take full advantage of that fact. One combat command would isolate the immobile 2nd Panzer in the Celles "pocket" and block the path of Panzer Lehr moving up from Bastogne to help. A second combat command was to throw a block on the 9th Panzer Division to the east before it could reach the tip of the salient.

Combat Command B came storming down on Celles on Christmas Day, split into two parts to envelop the main body of the 2nd Panzer in a forested area nearby, and then converged on the town itself. The German defenders were quickly routed, 200 of them surrendering. At the same time, the 2nd Panzer's reconnaissance battalion west of the town was surrounded. Hit from one direction by British armor donated by Field Marshal Montgomery, hit from another direction by Harmon's tanks, and bombed and strafed from the air, the battalion was cut to ribbons.

Without gasoline to counterattack or even to move, the 2nd Panzer's main body could only watch helplessly as Harmon laid his noose around it. Overhead, Allied fighter-bombers prowled patiently, pouncing on the slightest movement within the German pocket.

. Panzer Lehr and the 9th Panzer both tried to reach Celles during the day, but they were stopped cold by Harmon's armor and guns and by the ever-present Allied planes. That night, the reinforcing columns were ordered to pull back. The 2nd Panzer was left to its fate.

On Tuesday, December 26, 1944, the Battle of the Bulge reached its climax. Sepp Dietrich's Sixth Panzer Army was now reduced to a defensive role, stripped of its armor to shore up the salient to the west. Patton's tanks broke through to besieged Bastogne. And at Celles Ernie Harmon's "Hell on Wheels" tankers and infantrymen proceeded to take the 2nd Panzer Division apart.

It was deadly and methodical. First, U.S. artillery would batter a section of the heavily wooded pocket; moving up behind this curtain of shells, the infantry, backed by tanks and assault guns, mopped up the survivors. Then the whole operation was repeated on the next section of the steadily shrinking perimeter.

It took two days to clean out the Celles pocket, but the final victory was a complete one. Only 600 of the enemy were able to filter out of the pocket at night on foot. A total of 3,700 were killed, wounded, or captured; 82 tanks, 83 pieces of artillery, and almost 450 other vehicles were wrecked or captured. (The 2nd Armored's losses came to 17 killed, 227 wounded or missing, and 27 tanks.) After listing the spoils, Harmon summed up his report on the Battle of Celles in three words: "A great slaughter."

The Nazis, as Chester Wilmot put it, "had looked upon the Meuse for the last time." The Battle of the Bulge was far from over, but now its whole character was changing. For ten days Hitler's legions had held the initiative. On the eleventh day they lost it—permanently.

VI

THE LONG ROAD BACK

The climactic events of December 26, 1944, Ernie Harmon's victory at Celles and the relief of besieged Bastogne—marked the pivot point in the Battle of the Bulge. As relentlessly as an ocean tide, the struggle would now take a new direction. The war councils of both sides met to consider their next moves.

Adolf Hitler had left Eagle's Eyrie to return to Berlin, and on the 26th he held a long conference on Operation Christrose. The reports were grim—Dietrich's Sixth Panzer Army up against a stone wall along the northern front, Manteuffel's Fifth Panzer Army balked at Bastogne and along the Meuse, Brandenberger's Seventh Army flailing helplessly in the south. General Alfred Jodl, Hitler's fawning chief planning officer, summed up the outlook with unusual frankness. "Mein Führer," he said, "we must face the facts squarely and openly: we cannot force the Meuse."

Hitler, however, was still gripped by his fevered vision of an eleventh-hour victory in the West. "We have had unexpected setbacks—because my plan was not followed to the letter!" he raged. Brandenberger must regain the initiative in the south; Bastogne must be taken; Dietrich and Manteuffel must "wipe out the great Allied force we have caught in the bend of the Meuse"; Operation Nordwind, the offensive in Alsace, must not be delayed. Then the victory march would continue, across the Meuse and on to Antwerp.

Thus thousands more men were fated to die in the frozen, snowy wastes of the Ardennes. After the war, General Heinz Guderian, the German commander on the Eastern Front, attempted to explain Hitler's dark and tortured reasoning. "He had a special picture of the world," Guderian said. "Every fact had to fit in with that fancied picture. As he believed, so the world must be. But, in fact, it was a picture of another world."

As the Führer pursued his fanatic vision, the Allied high command was trying to hammer out a strategy of its own: exactly where and exactly when to counterattack. Among men as different as Eisenhower and Patton, Bradley and Montgomery, it was not an easy task.

On Christmas Day, with Patton's blessing, Bradley had flown to Montgomery's headquarters in Belgium to propose an immediate counteroffensive from north and south against the sides of the Bulge. He got nowhere at all. The Field Marshal insisted that the time was not yet ripe, that the Germans still held the initiative and would launch another assault in the north against the battered U.S. First Army. Seething, Bradley returned to his headquarters and set about trying to apply pressure on the Britisher.

First, he wrote to his friend Courtney Hodges, First Army commander, urging him to actively promote an offensive. Then, on the evening of December 26, Bradley telephoned Eisenhower's chief of staff, Lieutenant General Walter Bedell Smith. "Damn it, Bedell," he complained, "can't you people get Monty going on the north? As near as we can tell, this other fellow's reached his high-water mark today. He'll soon be starting to pull back—if not tonight, certainly tomorrow."

With Montgomery's reports in front of him, Smith disagreed. "Why, they'll be across the Meuse in forty-eight hours," he snapped back. Now thoroughly exasperated, convinced that the enemy was going to get away, Bradley could think of nothing more appropriate than Tony McAuliffe's remark. "Nuts!" he said, and hung up.

Dwight Eisenhower saw the situation much as Bradley and Patton saw it. But he also saw the need to smooth the growing friction between the Anglo-American allies. The result was a compromise. Montgomery gave up his original plan to counterattack just the tip of the German salient in favor of a strike farther east; but he won his point about timing. His offensive would not begin before January 3, 1945. In the meantime, the impatient Patton was allowed to begin his own attack northward from the Bastogne area.

By December 28, command decisions had been reached in Berlin and Belgium. Bradley need not have worried that the Germans would escape unharmed; both sides had decided on a strategy of attack. With the aim of cutting the Bulge in half, Hodges' First Army would strike south toward Houffalize, a town at almost the exact center of the battlefield. Patton's Third Army would come up from the south toward the same objective. For their part, Model and Manteuffel had made Bastogne their "central problem"—with a timetable of attack identical to Patton's.

George Patton was a driver, as offensive-minded a general as the U.S. Army possessed, but right now he was short of the tools of war. On the heels of its long, high-speed dash across France in the summer of 1944, the Third Army had become embroiled in heavy fighting in front of the Siegfried Line. These months of steady combat had left is equipment in poor condition. The armored divisions were all understrength, and their tanks were long over-due for maintenance. Over-used engines would not develop full power; faulty electrical systems forced tankers to crank their gun turrets around by hand; worn tracks and suspension systems broke in heavy going. One 4th Armored tank battalion, for example, had no less than thirty-three Shermans break down in the march north to the Ardennes.

As serious as the equipment problem was the shortage of infantry. The toll of battle had been greater than the flow of replacements to the Third Army, and the new men who had arrived needed more training to be effective soldiers. Instead, they found themselves thrown into the raging battle under the worst possible conditions.

To try to fill his thinned combat ranks, Patton resorted to combing behind-the-lines units—communications troops, engineers, anti-aircraft gunners, and the like—of ten per cent of their strength. The top ten per cent, he insisted. But very few officers had any intention of giving up their best men. In typical army fashion, they sent instead their "eight balls": the trouble-makers, the bumblers, the shirkers. Some of these men would turn into hard fighters in the coming battle; others turned and ran at the first shots.

Before he could launch any attack from the Bastogne salient, Patton had to lay certain essential groundwork. The first task was to anchor his right flank, the one facing the German Seventh Army. It was a bitter, plodding, bloody struggle. The German defenders made good use of the rugged terrain, just as the Americans had done in the early days of Operation Christrose. Slowly, however, the anchor was hammered home and the flank made secure.

The second task was to widen the corridor leading into Bastogne, which one weary 4th Armored GI described as "narrow enough to spit across". This job, too, was long and slow and hard. The Nazis had learned a great deal about wintertime fighting during their campaigns in Russia, and they put this knowledge to good use in the Ardennes. Their winter clothing, for example, was far better than the Americans, and they made more skillful use of camouflage. Nevertheless, by December 30, Patton had a solid base from which to begin his drive on Houffalize.

At 7:30 A.M. on the 30th, twin Third Army assault forces jumped off southeast and southwest of Bastogne, intending to sweep north past the town on both sides and close in on Houffalize. At exactly the same hour, General Manteuffel sent two powerful columns of his own against the sides of the Bastogne corridor to try to seal off the town again. These attacks, German and American, immediately smashed head-on into one another.

The western half of the battlefield exploded into a confused brawl. Two new U.S. divisions, one untested in battle and the other nearly as inexperienced, took a heavy pounding. The snowy fields were thick with fog and battle smoke, and men groped blindly for direction or dug frantically in the frozen ground to evade the incessant shelling. By the end of the day, both sides had lost many men and much armor and neither had made very much progress.

In the sector southeast of Bastogne, in the

vicinity of the village of Lutrebois, the veteran U.S. 35th Infantry Division was rocked back by the German assault but rallied and fought it to a standstill. Near Lutrebois, using "Indian tactics" with great skill, a half-dozen Shermans and a handful of tank destroyers ambushed a thrust by the 1st SS Panzer Division and wrecked nineteen Panthers and Tigers before the Germans knew what had hit them. A squadron of U.S. fighter-bombers popped out of the thickening weather to surprise another panzer force, sending it scurrying for cover.

The 35th Division sprang another surprise on Manteuffel's troops that day. The division artillery was trying out the so-called proximity fuze, a new top-secret electronic "sensing" device that detonated shells just before they struck their targets. This meant that the shells exploded with terrible effect directly over an enemy position rather than losing part of their force as they pounded into the ground. The badly shaken German troops dubbed these shells "tree smashers." There were far too few proximity fuzes yet available, but batteries that had them just about doubled the effectiveness of their fire.

The fighting around Bastogne on December 30 ended in a bloody stand-off. There would be no quick, bold thrust to Houffalize, as Patton and Bradley hoped. The Germans were going to stand and fight, gambling their reserves to regain the initiative. Back on December 19, at the American high command conference at Verdun, George Patton had claimed that "the

Kraut has stuck his head in a meat grinder" by coming out of the defenses of the Siegfried Line. Now Patton had the chance to make good his boast to "turn the handle."

As the old year ended and the new one began, the fight at Bastogne grew increasingly furious. The cruel weather took an ever greater toll. Infantrymen slogged through waist-deep drifts in near-zero temperatures. Wounded died in their foxholes of shock and exposure before medics could reach them. In some of the bloodiest fighting in the whole bloody Battle of the Bulge, desperate men struggled to villages or farm buildings simply to win warmth and shelter and a chance to eat a hot meal.

Always there was the fearful drama of life and death. American aid man Lester Atwell was on duty one night at a field hospital in a frigid Belgian barn when litter bearers brought in a wounded GI. "Everyone else crowded around," Atwell wrote, "but I did not want to see the wound. My one unwilling glance had shown a thin, dark boy, perhaps twenty years of age, with cheekbones standing out and dark, frightened eyes trying to focus, to understand where he was and what had happened to him....

"A group of us stumbled out. I remained outside the barn doors. A few minutes went by, then the captain and the five or six who were in the barn came out.

" 'God *damn* it!' someone was saying. 'Dead. He died....'

"The doctor kept muttering curses to himself and shaking his head. 'Goddam blood plasma was frozen! Couldn't thaw it out, couldn't *give* it to the guy....'

"A shock ran through me. In that short time, I thought, 'A life had gone out of earthly existence forever...a life that had been aimed like a guided missile at this moment, through childhood and school days, through the first pair of roller skates, the first two-wheel bike, through Christmases at home, through high school and baseball and first dates, to meet death here, frightened and bewildered, among strangers in a dark barn, on New Year's Eve in Belgium....'"

And into the picture-book Ardennes landscape continued to come the long columns of marching men, tired, unshaven, dirty men in American khaki and German field grey, past the frozen bodies of comrades sprawled in ditches and past the blackened hulks of burned-out tanks, half covered by fresh, sparkling snow.

On January 1, 1945, Hitler set in motion two surprise moves to try to save the battle slipping away from him. The first was Operation Nordwind, the attack in the Alsace region 125 miles south of the Ardennes. But the Allied 6th Army Group, under General Jacob Devers, was not caught napping. Americans and Frenchmen absorbed the blow with little trouble, and after a gain of less than fifteen miles, Nordwind sputtered out in failure. To Hitler's dismay, Jake Devers never needed to call on Patton for help to contain the threat.

The Führer's second surprise met with more

success—but in the end it, too, had no effect on the outcome of the Battle of the Bulge.

At first light on New Year's Day nearly every operational Luftwaffe fighter-bomber in the West—perhaps as many as a thousand of them, although the figures are hazy—streaked westward toward the Allied airfields in Belgium and Holland. Flying at treetop level to evade Allied air-warning radar, the German pilots found the kind of hunting they had only imagined in their wildest dreams: hundreds of American and British fighters and bombers and transport planes parked in neat rows around the edges of their fields.

In a matter of minutes the airstrips were smothered in clouds of oily black smoke and licking flames. Swarms of Messerschmitts and Focke-Wulfs swooped down to bomb and strafe, circled around, and came in again and again until their ammunition was exhausted. Then they departed as suddenly as they appeared.

"I gave the order to regroup," a Luftwaffe pilot recalled. "Then one more glance at the smoking piles of debris and the occasional columns of flames. The snow had melted and dirty grey pools of water had formed between the burning aircraft. One solitary ack-ack crew fired in vain as we left...."

At one field near Brussels, 123 Spitfire and Typhoon fighters, C-47 transports, and Flying Fortress heavy bombers were wrecked beyond repair. The final toll came to nearly 300 American and British aircraft. The Germans lost some ninety planes to anti-aircraft fire and to the Allied fighters that managed to get into the air.

This "ugly surprise," as an Air Force historian described it, paralyzed Allied airpower in the Ardennes for a week. Then new planes poured in from England to make good the losses. Like Operation Nordwind, the Luftwaffe's New Year's Day strike ever, the American outposts frantically warned of a German counterattack. The roar of motors came from the direction of Flamierge, and then heavy tanks clattered slowly down the road, their turrets turning, the long cannon probing for the American positions. White-suited infantry trailed along behind them. Without armor of their own, the paratroopers suddenly became simply men pitted against terrifying machines. A withdrawal was ordered.

Raked by the cannon and machine guns of the panzers, the GI's raced back across the same field they had won so painfully the day before. Scores did not make it, falling, screaming in the drifts. The rest ran on, gasping for breath, throwing off their heavy packs. At last they reached the cover of the woods from which they had begun their attack. Of the 200 men in the company, only twenty returned to their start line. Flamierge and its vital road remained in German hands.

Only slowly, ever so slowly, was the stalemate broken. Patton and Hodges relentlessly pressed their attacks, levering more men and guns and tanks into the offensive. By January 8, the U.S. northern and southern spearheads were barely a dozen miles apart. Blunt reports poured into Berlin, warning Hitler that unless an immediate retreat was ordered, complete disaster was inevitable; seven of Model's panzer divisions and thousands upon thousands of his troops were still west of Houffalize.

The Führer at last faced the stark reality. His great dream—the Meuse, Antwerp, the collapse of the Western Allies—was dead. Operation Christrose had failed. He authorized a withdrawal.

To the Germans west of Houffalize it was now a question of simple defeat or total annihilation. Their columns inched eastward toward the narrowing Houffalize gap. Vehicles that broke down or ran out of fuel had to be abandoned; soon the snowy roads were lined with scores of the tanks and guns so carefully hoarded for the great offensive. The infantry plodded on, numb with cold and fatigue and sickness.

The Americans redoubled their efforts to spring the trap. Some 15,000 Nazi paratroopers were squeezed in a vise by three of Patton's divisions and decimated. (That same day, January 12, the Russians opened a massive offensive on the Eastern Front, tearing great gaps in the thin German lines.) As Houffalize came within range of Hodges' artillery, its narrow streets became a maelstrom of bursting shells and burning vehicles and running men. German rear guards fought with suicidal courage to hold the escape route open.

On the evening of January 15, Patton ordered

Stephen W. Sears

reconnaissance units to slip northward through enemy lines to Houffalize to make contact with the First Army. One of these units was Task Force Greene, 450 men in light tanks, armored cars, half-tracks, and jeeps, led by Major Michael Greene.

The column ground along a forest trail in the ominously silent darkness, expecting to be ambushed at any moment. At dawn, in sight of Houffalize, it was discovered. A fierce fire fight drove the Germans off. Then a column of men was spotted on a ridge to the north. A patrol was sent out to investigate.

Soon it was back, the men bursting with the news. "That's the 2nd Armored up there!" the patrol leader exclaimed to Major Greene.

Task Force Greene was one of several units to make contact with Hodges' troops in those early morning hours; which contact was the first was a matter of some dispute. In any case, the First and Third armies had joined hands, forming a solid front and slicing the Bulge in half. Although some 20,000 Germans were cut off to the west, the majority of Model's troops in the tip of the salient had slipped through the jaws of the trap before they snapped shut. It was January 16, 1945—one month almost to the hour after Operation Christrose had begun.

The enormous drama of the Ardennes was all but over. For the surviving German troops only one thought remained: to reach the comparative safety of the Siegfried Line.

"Rivers of men and machines flowed slowly toward the Fatherland," wrote historian John

108

Toland. "Great lines of trucks, tanks, and self-propelled guns rumbled east over icy roads and trails clogged with snowdrifts. Long, discouraged lines of infantrymen trudged in the powdery snow, pursued by death from the Americans or the bitter weather....

"The will of the German soldier was broken. No one that survived the retreat believed there was the slightest chance of German victory. Each refugee of the Battle of the Bulge brought home a story of doom, of overwhelming Allied might, and of the terrible weapon forged in the Ardennes: the American fighting man...."

VII

RECKONING OF BATTLE

Following the decisive link-up of the American First and Third armies at Houffalize on January 16, 1945, the fighting in the Ardennes became part of the relentless Allied drive to reach and cross the Rhine River, Nazi Germany's final line of defense in the West. On January 23, St. Vith was recaptured—fittingly enough, by the U.S. 7th Armored Division that had defended it so fiercely. By the end of January the last traces of the Bulge were erased.

In 1939 Adolf Hitler had set out to conquer and humble the great powers of Western civilization. Time and again the deadly combination of swift panzers, disciplined infantry, and the Luftwaffe had taken the offensive, carrying the Führer frighteningly close to his goal. Operation Christrose was the last of these great offensives;

its failure marked the final failure of the Nazi dream of world conquest. Just over three months later, in May, 1945, Hitler's Thousand-Year Reich expired in an agony of death and devastation.

That January, however, as the Bulge was slowly and painfully whittled away, the measure of victory and defeat in the Ardennes was not yet clear. The Germans had indeed been halted and beaten back. But just by taking the offensive, had they achieved at least a partial victory?

In terms of his ultimate goal—a decisive victory that would force the Western Allies into a negotiated peace —Hitler of course failed utterly. In terms of the more realistic goals of such German field commanders as Model and Manteuffel—pushing the Americans back beyond the Meuse and inflicting crippling casualties on them in the process—they, too, failed, although only narrowly. In the fight for time, however, the Nazis appeared to have won a victory. General Eisenhower admitted that his plan for the final Anglo-American offensive had been set back by some six weeks.

In the end even that victory was an illusion. Hitler's gamble in the West opened wide the floodgates in the East. The thinning of German forces on the Eastern Front, the assignment of nearly all new tanks and guns and planes to support Christrose, and the commitment of the German Army's last reserves in the Ardennes greatly eased the path of the Russian offensive that opened on January 12. With a superiority in men and armor of at least six to one, the Russian armies surged westward. In the first week they gained 100 miles; in the second week, 120 miles. By late January, as the last of Model's troops were driven out of the Bulge, the Russians were across the eastern frontier of the German homeland. Without question, the life of Hitler's Third Reich was shortened by the battle in the Ardennes.

(There is a final irony to Hitler's gamble. In the unlikely event that Christrose *had* achieved a major success, prolonging the life of the Third Reich, the end result would likely have been apocalyptic destruction. The American development of the atomic bomb, originally undertaken to be used against the Nazis, was far enough along that it could have been dropped on Hitler's Germany by early August of 1945.)

The defeat of Nazism's last offensive was achieved only at a terrible cost. American casualties totaled nearly 77,000 men—8,600 killed, 47,000 wounded, 21,000 missing or captured. The loss of armor—733 tanks and tank destroyers—was especially severe. Troy Middleton's VIII Corps bore the heaviest losses: the 28th and 106th divisions wrecked, one combat command of the 9th Armored Division all but wiped out. But every Allied division engaged in the Ardennes suffered wounds slow to heal.

There is no certain knowledge of German losses, owing to conflicting and incomplete records. The best guess is a figure somewhere between 100,000 and 120,000 men, and 300 to 400 tanks. There is certainty on one point, however: these were losses that Germany, in the sixth year of war, simply could not make good. The German Army was broken beyond recovery in the Ardennes.

Whatever light history has cast on the Battle of the Bulge, its immediate harvest was a bitterness so strong that even today it has not entirely disappeared.

Part of that bitterness grew out of the fact that the battle took place at all. In the seven months or so between June 6, 1944, the date of the Anglo-American invasion of France, and December 16, the people of Great Britain and the United States had been cheered by news of one spectacular victory after another. Far from the realities of the battlefield, deeply involved in the fate of husbands, brothers, and sons on the battle fronts, they prayed for a quick end to the struggle. What they read in their newspapers and heard on their radios during those months led them to believe that their prayers were soon to be answered.

Then came the news from the Ardennes. The shock to morale was enormous. All the old fears of Nazi might, so deeply ingrained in the early years of the war, came flooding back. How could this happen? Why had the Allies been caught napping? Who was to blame?

The truth of the matter is that the complexities of modern warfare were beyond the grasp of those on the home front. The staggering volume of supplies needed to maintain the seven Allied armies as they neared the German border; the difficulties of obtaining enough men and equipment to build up the required superiority of offense over defense to keep the initiative; the hampering effects of terrain and weather—these and a hundred other problems beset Dwight Eisenhower and his high command. Choices had to be made, compromises accepted: that, after all, is what the so-called art of war is all about. And so the "unprofitable" Ardennes sector was lightly held in order to attack far more profitable objectives to the north and south.

Another reality of modern warfare: by taking the great gamble of committing the cream of his army, equipping it with his best weapons, and throwing in the bulk of his reserves, Adolf Hitler was bound to achieve some sort of breakthrough. The failure of Allied Intelligence to detect the impending offensive made the breakthrough worse than it might otherwise have been. Still, an offensive as powerful as Operation Christrose could not have been easily stopped under the best of circumstances. The wonder of the Battle of the Bulge was not what the Nazis achieved but the fact that they were contained and finally broken as soon as they were. That Germany could not finally afford the price it paid for attacking is the true measure of the American victory in the Ardennes.

A second crop of bitterness grew out of what one historian of the battle has called "the soil of human vanity."

Adolf Hitler had hoped to split the Anglo-American coalition with a victory in battle. Ironically, that split nearly occurred in a war of words. The center of controversy was Field Marshal Bernard Montgomery.

Militarily, Montgomery made vital contributions to victory. Being a superb military "housekeeper," he brought much needed order to the chaotic northern half of the battlefield. After he took command, the troops under him began to fight according to an over-all plan, rather than simply reacting to the enemy's moves. With Montgomery in charge, British forces were brought in to help sooner than they might have been had an American been given the command.

His careful caution is more debatable. It certainly prevented some of the over-impetuous U.S. generals from getting into hot water by counterattacking too soon. On the other hand, Lightning Joe Collins' decision to attack the 2nd Panzer Division at Celles on December 25, a decision taken against the spirit of the Field Marshal's orders, quickly and firmly checked the German offensive short of the Meuse. It may be that Montgomery never quite appreciated the initiative and the pride of the men he was commanding.

In any case, none of this was worth arguing about for very long. But then Montgomery proceeded to indulge his old habit of utter tactlessness. The result was inter-Allied fireworks.

First he took advantage of the new command set-up to renew his old argument with Supreme Commander Eisenhower over the whole strategy of the European campaign. Ever since the landings in Normandy, Montgomery had been arguing for one single narrow thrust into Germany (which he expected to command) and against Eisenhower's strategy of an advance on a broad front. When he opened up the issue again in the midst of the Ardennes crisis, Eisenhower's hot temper, normally sheathed in patience and good humor, exploded. He let Montgomery know that if he kept this up, "one of us will have to go." He made it equally clear that he doubted that the two Allied governments would choose to replace the Supreme Commander. Montgomery dropped the matter.

Then, on January 7, as the twin thrusts on Houffalize ground agonizingly ahead, the Field Marshal called a press conference. He described for the reporters how he had taken charge of a situation that "looked as if it might become awkward" and how he had gone about "tidying up the battlefield." After more in this vein, he summed up the battle as "one of the most interesting and tricky I have ever handled."

In saying these things, Montgomery left the impression that he had been called upon to rescue the Americans from a mess of their own making and that the turning of the tide of battle was due largely to his efforts and his efforts alone. He neglected to note that the assignment to him of two of Bradley's armies was only temporary; nor did he even once mention Bradley's name. The newspapers, especially the British newspapers, picked up this theme and elaborated upon it. Now it was the turn of Bradley and Patton to explode.

Eventually this crack in the Anglo-American coalition was papered over and the various ruffled feathers were smoothed. No other such incident of the war, Eisenhower later wrote, "caused me more distress and worry." It remained for British Prime Minister Winston Churchill, that most realistic and eloquent of statesmen, to put the matter into proper perspective.

"Care must be taken in telling our proud tale," Churchill advised his nation, "not to claim for the British armies undue share of what is undoubtedly the greatest American battle of the war and will, I believe, be regarded as an ever-famous American victory.... We must not forget that it is to American homes that telegrams of personal loss and anxiety have been coming during the past month and that there has been a hard and severe ordeal during these weeks for our brave and cherished ally.... Let no one lend themselves to the shouting of mischief makers when issues of this momentous consequence are being successfully decided by sword."

So the furor finally died down, but the bitterness remained—to be kept alive by armchair strategists and by the generals refighting the battle in their memoirs after the war.

Perhaps the deepest stain on the memory of the Battle of the Bulge was the one imprinted by Nazi savagery. The Malmédy Massacre set the pattern. As the German tide was rolled back, more and more details of brutality and murder were uncovered. In the village of Bande, within the tip of the Bulge, British soldiers found the bodies of thirty-two young men, some of them seminary students, killed by the Gestapo in revenge for the village's role in the resistance movement during the earlier German occupation. Along the bloody trail of Kampfgruppe Peiper the frozen corpses of scores more GI prisoners of war were discovered, murdered by their SS captors. In the town of Stavelot alone, ninety-two civilians died at the hands of the SS.

In 1946 Joachim Peiper and Sepp Dietrich and sixty-five of their men were tried and convicted of crimes against prisoners and civilians during the battle. The trial, however, was a travesty of American justice, with beatings, forced confessions, and dishonest testimony. After several investigations, the two German officers were released from prison a decade later. This unfortunate affair resulted in some of the guilty escaping punishment, some of the innocent suffering for crimes they did not commit, and a further legacy of bitterness.

There is far more to the final reckoning of the Battle of the Bulge, however, than simply bitter memories. Time has confirmed Winston Churchill's judgment that it would be remembered beyond all else as "an ever-famous American victory."

There were many contributions to that victory—the quick and decisive actions of Dwight Eisenhower and his generals, the rapid marshaling of reinforcements, the expert handling of the U.S. artillery, the intervention of the Allied air forces, to name a few. But in the last analysis, the destruction of Operation Christrose was due to the courage and tenacity of the American GI.

The greatest mistake Adolf Hitler made was to underestimate the fighting quality of the U.S. soldier. Like his forefathers in the Revolution and the Civil War and World War I, the average GI of World War II was at heart a civilian in arms. He cared little about the professional soldier's war-like bearing. He was careless about military spit and polish, casual about discipline, irreverent toward authority, and he did as little military house-keeping as he thought he could get away with. In his contempt for such "softness and decadence," Hitler utterly failed to see the fierce pride that was in the American fighting man. When the going was tough—and the going in the Ardennes was very tough indeed—the GI used his wits and his initiative and his independence of mind with an effectiveness that few soldiers in any of the world's armies could match.

The American soldier had no monopoly on courage. But in those dark and savage days in the Ardennes he revealed, beyond courage, an extra steel-hard quality of mind and spirit that turned one of America's greatest battles into one of America's greatest victories.